OTHER

Harlequin Romances

by SARA SEALE

Many of these titles are available at your local bookseller, or through the Harlequin Reader Service.

For a free catalogue listing all available Harlequin Romances, send your name and address to:

HARLEQUIN READER SERVICE,
M.P.O. Box 707, Niagara Falls, N.Y. 14302
Canadian address: Stratford, Ontario, Canada.

or use order coupon at back of book.

THE UNKNOWN
MR. BROWN

by

SARA SEALE

HARLEQUIN BOOKS   TORONTO
WINNIPEG

Original hard cover edtion published in 1971
by Mills & Boon Limited, 17 - 19 Foley Street,
London W1A 1DR, England
under the title "Mr. Brown"

© Sara Seale 1971

Harlequin edition published May, 1972

SBN 373-01597-6

Printed in Canada

CHAPTER ONE

IT had seemed a long time to the impatient schoolgirl waiting in the outer office of Messrs. Chapple, Chapple & Ponsonby's city premises on the occasion of that first extraordinary interview before the elderly clerk ushered her into the presence of the senior partner.

"I'm Victoria Mary Hayes," she had announced confidingly almost before the door had closed behind her. "Are *you* Mr. Brown?"

The benevolent-looking old gentleman who was rising to greet her paused half-way and sat down again, his deceptive air of bonhomie momentarily vanishing behind an expression of prim disapproval.

"Certainly not," he replied, sounding faintly shocked. "And I might remind you, young lady, that the identity of your—er—benefactor is no concern of yours. You are very unlikely to meet."

"Oh!" She sounded both disappointed and justly reproved, but the next minute had returned to the attack with, he thought, a most improper want of respect. "But it sounds so unlikely. Complete strangers don't adopt you out of the blue, and if they did they would surely want to have a look at you first—not buying a pig in a poke, if you see what I mean."

"Mr. Brown has *not* adopted you, as we've been at some pains to point out in our correspondence," the lawyer retorted a little sharply. "As to having a look at you, as you rather baldly put it, I have already explained that he saw you in court and for reasons best known to himself decided on this rather unusual course of action. Since he has followed the case he is quite aware of your history. Whether he is—er—buying a pig in a poke will be up to you," he added with a somewhat wintry smile. "It would seem that, unlike counsel for the prosecution, he was—er—not unmoved by your evidence."

"Counsel for the prosecution was too busy having a ball at my expense to worry about my feelings. He got

5

a kick out of every minute of it," she retorted with some venom, and he frowned.

"My dear child! Robert Farmer is too able and too experienced in cross-examination to—er—get a kick out of making mincemeat of a schoolgirl," he said with some sharpness. "In my opinion, you should never have been called in the first place, and had Farmer been defending he would not have made that mistake. Your evidence did your father no good."

"No," she answered quietly, sounding suddenly grave and older than her fourteen years, "they told me afterwards I had let him down. You see, Mr. Chapple, I hadn't understood that I must give prearranged answers even if they weren't strictly true."

"Yes, well . . . your evidence was clearly ill-prepared, but it's all over now and at least you will not have to suffer for your father's mistakes," the lawyer said rather testily, but he observed her uneasily across the imposing width of his desk. She sat there staring beyond him at the impressive rows of deedboxes, looking as she had looked that day in the witness-box, withdrawn to the point of stupidity, with those wide blue eyes staring blankly over Counsel's shoulder. She was too thin and her face was all angles with ears that were not only a peculiar shape but seemed to be much too large, and he wondered what young Farmer, who was said to have an eye for the ladies, had made of her when he rose to cross-examine. He had dealt with her gently enough to begin with, mindful of Mr. Justice Seldon's well-known prejudices in the matter of children giving evidence, but she had proved a stubborn and argumentative witness and Farmer could hardly be blamed for a little rough handling towards the end.

It had been an unsavoury case altogether, Mr. Chapple reflected distastefully, uncovering shady financial transactions which had put several small firms out of business. Grahame Hayes had been a dupe rather than a principal and might have got off lightly, but the defence had been mishandled and he made a bad impression in the box. The court had adjourned, leaving the judge's summing up for the morrow. Bail having been granted upon a large security, Hayes had returned to his home but, unable to face a prison sentence, he had taken an overdose which, if unsatisfactory from the point of view of justice, at least saved the country expense, thought Mr. Chapple with his usual cynicism.

It had been tough on the girl of course. The mother had been dead for some years and there were no relations to offer a home or financial security. The expensive education her father had planned for her would certainly have come to nothing but for the whim of an eccentric client with more money than sense and a taste for playing providence, thought Mr. Chapple.

"Well now," he said briskly, "returning to Mr. Brown . . . have you quite understood this situation?"

"Understood what?" she asked vaguely.

"The arrangements that have been made for your future," the lawyer replied impatiently. Really! The child could look almost half-witted at times with that wide, unblinking stare and the mousy hair dragged back from those prominent ears, giving her a skinned appearance.

"Oh, yes," she answered with rather disconcerting composure. "A Trust has been formed which operates until I'm twenty-one. I'm to finish my education along the lines my father had laid down, spend the holidays at places appointed by Mr. Brown, apply to this office for money when necessary, send periodical reports of progress to Mr. Brown and be responsible to Mr. Brown for good behaviour. I suppose," she added with a sudden grin, "there really *is* a Mr. Brown?"

"Oh, yes, my client exists and will expect a reckoning," he assured her with a heavy attempt at roguishness, "so don't run away with the idea that you can play ducks and drakes with his money, young lady."

She gave him a long, considering look as she got up slowly, smoothing down her brief skirt with unchildlike carefulness, then she bestowed upon him that unexpected slow, rather beguiling smile which, he remembered, had momentarily halted Counsel in the early stages of his cross-examination.

"I think I've learnt my lesson regarding other people's money, Mr. Chapple," she said in a cool little voice and, for almost the first time in his professional career, he found himself put out of countenance. He did not like

7

the girl, he decided uncomfortably, and understood very well what had prompted Robert Farmer's subsequent harshness.

"My dear child, I had no intention—I was merely using a colloquialism—the sort of—er—avuncular jest not intended to be taken seriously," he said, rather red in the face, heaving his corpulent figure out of his chair with some effort.

"That's quite all right, Mr. Chapple. No hard feelings," she told him kindly, then suddenly reverted to her proper age. "Mr. Brown must be stinking rich— stinking rich and slightly bats, wouldn't you say?" she observed. "That isn't his real name, of course, is it?"

"It's the name my client chooses to be known by. As to your other assumption, had I observed any sign of—er—derangement, I would scarcely have been a party to such an undertaking," he replied rather pompously.

"No, I suppose not. Still, you must admit it all sounds a bit cock-eyed—unless, of course, he had something to do with my father's trouble and is salving his conscience. Is he—salving his conscience, I mean?"

Mr. Chapple's countenance assumed a purple tinge.

"That is a most improper suggestion," he snapped severely.

"Improper? I don't understand. I wasn't suggesting that the old gentleman was indecent, or anything."

He shot her a suspicious glance, resolving firmly to delegate future interviews to one of his partners, but she was gazing at him with what appeared to be honest perplexity and he cleared his throat gustily.

"Merely a legal use of the term and not intended to imply—er—indecency—however, you will be well advised to check your quite natural curiosity," he told her, his hand already on the bell which would summon his clerk. "Your—er—benefactor has particularly stressed that he wishes to remain anonymous, neither does he desire any personal contact with you. Just think of him as someone in the background holding a watching brief for you which, if I may say so without offence, is more than you could rightly expect in the—er—circumstances."

"Oh, I entirely agree with you," she said obligingly,

edging towards the door. "If it wasn't for this mysterious Mr. Brown I would be begging my bread in the streets like the unfortunate heroines in our cook's favourite romances." She paused at the door as a fresh thought struck her. "Perhaps I remind him of someone he has lost, which of course would explain things — a much loved only daughter?"

"As far as I am aware, Mr. Brown is unmarried," he replied somewhat stiffly, then aware that even this much information was a breach of professional etiquette, he pressed his bell with determined finality.

She looked surprised but made no comment, then apologising politely for taking up so much of his valuable time, departed abruptly without waiting for the clerk to show her out.

Now, four years later, Victoria found herself travelling to the same destination on the top of a city-bound bus, summoned at last to a meeting with Mr. Brown. He had assumed so many different disguises through the imaginative years of her schooldays that she told herself the reality was sure to be a let-down. Whether he was a crusty recluse who had been crossed in love, or a reformed criminal expiating his past through charity, or just a rich eccentric with a taste for power, she owed him the security which her father had planned for her and she hoped he would not regret his munificence when they met.

She had been accustomed for so long to her situation that she had ceased to regard it as strange. She had, as required, written regularly to Mr. Brown, stiff, impersonal little letters, dutifully reporting progress in her studies and receiving in due course brief acknowledgements from Chapple, Chapple & Ponsonby. She wished that Mr. Brown would sometimes reply in person, but he never did, neither despite vague promises, had he ever attended prize-givings or end-of-term theatricals, occasions when the presence of parents and guardians afforded much consequence to the participants.

The London house had been sold to meet the demands of creditors, but the week-end bungalow in the country had been retained for the period of her schooling, and here the holidays had been spent with Dora Scott, her father's one-time secretary who had dealt with his private affairs and run his house ever since he had become a widower.

Upon leaving school Victoria had been against the doubtful advantages of being finished abroad.

"It's silly these days when most girls are finding jobs and saving their parents unnecessary expense," she had told Scottie, "and specially so in my case. When the Trust is finally wound up, I'll presumably have to earn a living, so why waste time and Mr. Brown's money playing at being a future deb? It's time I met this Mr. Brown and put him wise. Who do you think he is, Scottie? One of Father's less respectable cronies doing penance?"

"I've no idea. Your father had many contacts in all walks of life. Any one of them might conceivably be repaying a favour and, whoever he may be, it doesn't do to look a gift horse in the mouth. At least he's giving you the start in life your father had planned for you."

"Well, things have changed since then and I've done with school now. Far better to send me to some training college where I can learn something useful instead of wasting time being groomed for social occasions which I'm never likely to grace."

"Well, why don't you write and suggest it?" Scottie had said to end the argument, and Victoria had. She not only firmly stated her views, but intimated that it was time she was summoned to a personal interview with Mr. Brown. And summoned she had been to attend the offices of Messrs. Chapple, Chapple & Ponsonby at eleven-thirty on the following Friday when her remarks would be given attention. So here she was, riding on the top of a bus, her anticipation mounting with every mile, determined to like and even to love Mr. Brown in whatever guise he should present himself.

The bus halted to set down passengers outside the Law Courts and she watched the gowned and bewigged figures hurrying to and fro amongst the loitering sightseers, sharply reminded of her own unhappy experience. She could look back now on that brief interruption in the ordered pattern of her schooldays with discomfort rather than sorrow, but as she gazed down upon those forbidding halls of justice, certain faces rose clearly in her mind as if she had seen them yesterday. Her father, pale and uneasy, sporting the inevitable carnation in his buttonhole and refusing to catch her eye, the judge heavily aloof on his bench, looking rather like a sad, elderly bloodhound whose drooping ears had turned grey, and the thin-lipped, ironic face of the prosecuting counsel as he stripped her of dignity and assurance. She had little recollection of Counsel for the Defence who had taken her so gently through the preliminaries, but Robert Farmer's face with its fastidious, chiselled look, cold and colourless as the dusty grey of his wig, she would remember always with that same hurt resentment she had felt as a child. Until the advent of Mr. Brown had directed her fancies into other channels it had afforded her pleasure to invent crushing defeats for Mr. Farmer, even bodily harm, and she had been delighted to learn from the gossip columns in the Sunday press that his engagement to some well-known socialite had been broken off on the very eve of marriage. It had been distinctly soothing to the spirit to picture Mr. Farmer suffering the pangs of unrequited love, and although by now he had probably married someone else, Victoria still liked to imagine that things had turned out badly for him.

The bus dropped her within minutes of her destination and as she mounted the dark staircase to the first floor, the same musty smell of ancient archives greeted her and in the outer office the elderly clerk regarded her over his spectacles with the same air of faint disapproval.

"I don't suppose you remember me?" she said gaily, hoping to astonish with her newly acquired emancipation, but he replied with a discouraging lack of surprise as he rose from his desk:

"Certainly I remember you, Miss Hayes. Please be seated. Mr. Ponsonby will see you in a few minutes."

She had not met Mr. Ponsonby and for a moment forgot that he was a partner in the firm.

"Is that his real name?" she asked eagerly, and felt reproved once more by the chilly glance the old man bestowed on her.

"It is not the custom of this firm to shelter behind false identities when receiving clients," he replied coldly, and she gave a small, nervous giggle.

"I thought you meant Mr. Brown," she said, feeling both foolish and disappointed.

"Indeed?" he countered with raised eyebrows, then a buzzer sounded with peremptory impatience and he rose to his feet.

"Mr. Ponsonby will see you now, miss," he murmured, and ushered her over to one of the closed doors which separated the office from the partners' private rooms.

True to his previous resolution, Mr. Chapple had delegated this interview to his junior partner, and Mr. Ponsonby rose to receive his client with only a faint flicker of curiosity in the gaze which he allowed to dwell on her with momentary appraisal.

"Well now, Miss Hayes, come and sit down and let's hear your objections to our arrangements for you," he said, indicating a chair by the desk. "An opportunity to round off your education abroad isn't given to many these hard times, I may say."

"For that very reason—" she began, then her eyes came to rest on a door at the far end of the room. "Is he in there?" she asked.

"Mr. Chapple is in occupation, naturally, but he is busy with a client. Did you wish to see him particularly?" Mr. Ponsonby replied.

"Not Mr. Chapple. Mr. Brown," said Victoria impatiently, and the little lawyer's rather sparse eyebrows climbed up his forehead.

"Mr.—er—Brown is not on the premises as far as I am aware," he said with some surprise. "Had you expected to see him?"

"Yes—yes, I had. He was obviously the person to discuss my future with and—from the way your letter was worded, I thought—"

"In that case, there must have been some slight error in the drafting," Mr. Ponsonby interrupted with a thin smile. "Mr. Brown had no appointment with us, and merely gave instructions to deal with any queries as we saw fit. Now—" he glanced at his watch yet again "—if you would state your reasons for requesting this interview we can clear up any little misunderstanding and set your mind at rest."

"You can set my mind at rest best by letting me talk to Mr. Brown," she answered stubbornly. "Why do I never meet him?"

"Mr. Brown is a very busy person. He has many commitments."

"Such as?"

"Oh, this and that. His interests cover a wide field."

"Who is he, Mr. Ponsonby? Surely you can tell me that much?"

"I am not in a position to say," the lawyer replied stiffly and, as it happened, with perfect truth.

Victoria sighed, feeling not only disappointed, but cheated into the bargain. She had been so sure that this summons to the solicitors' office was in the nature of a rendezvous, but it looked very much as if the elusive Mr. Brown was determined to remain a myth.

On being pressed again to state her objections to their arrangements, she did so, but her old assurance had deserted her, knowing the battle to be lost already. Mr. Ponsonby swept aside her ill-expressed opinions with tolerant amusement, read her a short homily on the need to accept good fortune with grace, and pointed out somewhat acidly that most young women in her position would jump at the chance for betterment and not confuse the issue with foolish fancies.

"In other words, don't look a gift horse in the mouth," said Victoria, remembering Scottie's crisp retort to her protests.

"Exactly," Mr. Ponsonby observed with satisfaction, and rose hastily to his feet after another and more pointed look at his watch. "Now, everything is quite clear in your mind, I trust. Arrangements have already been made with the Paris end and the excellent Miss Scott has her instructions regarding travel and any personal requirements,

13

so you have nothing to worry about. One day, my dear young lady, you will be grateful for these advantages."

"Perhaps," she agreed politely but without conviction. "I can only hope that if I ever do get around to meeting Mr. Brown, he will feel he's had his money's worth."

So Victoria had completed the educational programme laid down for her and the faceless image of Mr. Brown receded once more into the background. She dutifully resumed the obligatory correspondence, reporting progress, and trying to convey her impressions of this new life in more colourful terms than the stilted accounts of her schooldays in England, but it was difficult to maintain contact with a person one had never met and who never replied, and her letters became briefer and duller as time went on.

And so the year had slipped away with so much to offer that was new and delightful that the days seemed scarcely long enough. Victoria made few intimate friends among her fellow pupils who seemed to be always newly arrived, or finished and leaving, transformed at great expense into polished young ladies ready to reward their parents' efforts by attracting suitable husbands. Sometimes she wondered whether the unknown Mr. Brown was conducting some cranky experiment and had some such plans for her, but it seemed unlikely unless he was proposing to take her into his home and launch her upon society, which was more unlikely still.

All too soon the time had approached when she, like the other girls, would be packing up to go home, and her thoughts turned once more to the question of earning a living. She could not feel that the social accomplishments insisted upon by Madame would stand her in much stead with prospective employers when set against a lack of more rudimentary abilities. Deportment and a sense of chic were all very well for those destined to grace society, but for her, a course at a training college might have been more useful. Still, she was emancipated enough now to be grateful for that year of leisurely transition from child to adult. Her French was very passable, she could discuss the

Arts intelligently, and she had learnt discrimination in the choice of food and wine. If she did not rate herself very highly in the matter of chic, having only a passing interest in fashion, she had learnt to make the best of her appearance.

Altogether, thought Victoria, having completed an assessment of her possible assets with modest satisfaction, she had not done too badly by Mr. Brown, though it seemed a pity to have acquired the superficial trappings of a finished young lady when there seemed little chance of profiting by them.

She would, she supposed, be returning to the bungalow and Scottie's chaperonage until such time when Mr. Brown should consider her competent to earn a living but it was Scottie herself who determined the immediate future. She was, she wrote, shortly to go into hospital for an operation, and since convalescence was likely to be lengthy, and it was not considered suitable for Victoria to live alone, the bungalow was to be let furnished temporarily. The lawyers were making arrangements with a small hostel in the Swiss Alps which took in a few advanced students for a limited period during the winter sports season, and Victoria must consider herself fortunate that such an opportunity should come her way.

The first weeks in that small, unfashionable winter resort high up in the Alps were a revelation, for after the discreet supervision of Madame's select establishment, the freedom provided by the little hostel was both unexpected and stimulating. Victoria proved herself an apt pupil in the arts of skiing and skating and although, as in Paris, she made few intimate friends of her own age, she became pleasurably acquainted with a young widow who was stopping at the nearby hotel with her small rather delicate son in hopes that he would benefit by the invigorating mountain air.

The boy, who was slightly lame, had taken an immediate fancy to Victoria who he seemed to regard as not very much older than his own five years, and an attachment sprang up between all three.

"You should be flattered. Timmy isn't given to crushes,"

15

Kate Allen had said at one of their early meetings, but did not add that she herself had felt drawn to this solitary girl with the enquiring eyes and delicately angled face, looking so impossibly slender in her tight black ski suit.

Victoria had been not only flattered but ready to return the compliment in full measure. Timmy, flaxen-haired and smoothly pink, had engaging ways. She thought his mother fussed a little unduly, but upon learning later something of Kate's history she supposed it was only natural. Jim Allen had been tragically killed in a motor accident before his son was born and Kate who had been with him blamed herself bitterly, not only for insisting on accompanying him against his better judgment, but for the child's slight infirmity which she believed to be a direct result. Kate, who had taken to inviting the girl over to the hotel for tea or aperitifs, was never very forthcoming about her own affairs, but Victoria understood that she had been left rather badly off and now lived in an old Sussex farmhouse and wrote books for children to augment her income. It seemed a little sad to Victoria that Kate with her gift for home-making and regrets for the denial of other children should resign herself to widowhood at the early age of thirty, but although she was too sensitive to another's reserve to elicit confidences that were not freely offered, she hoped very much there was some man in Kate's life who was waiting to fill the gap.

Kate, on the other hand, soon knew all about her Mr. Brown, and his strange beneficence. She remembered the Hayes scandal, but the case had made little impression on her at the time, coinciding as it had with her own personal tragedy, and had only been brought to mind by a casual reference before she left England, suggesting that she might get acquainted should she happen to run across the girl.

Christmas had come and gone and with it many of the tourists and soon Victoria realised with a pang, the Allens would be leaving, too. The boy had certainly benefited from the mountain air but, said Kate a shade wryly, it was time she got down to work again and replenished her dwindling coffers.

They were sitting on the terrace of the small hotel watching the beginners on the nursery slopes staggering about and falling down, Victoria with amused recollection of her own first efforts. She had progressed quickly to better things, being light and supple with an excellent sense of balance, thanks, no doubt, to Madame's tedious insistence on deportment, but for her, too, the interlude was coming to an end and only that morning she had received disturbing news from Scottie. Although the operation had been over and done with months ago, convalescence had been retarded with several small setbacks, and now Scottie wrote from the nursing home to which she had once more returned, explaining with her usual calm acceptance that as it was considered likely that she would remain a semi-invalid for the rest of her life, it would seem wise in the circumstances to accept her sister's offer of a permanent home in Wales. She had already informed the solicitors who would be making fresh arrangements for Victoria, and although she much regretted being unable to complete her undertaking with Mr. Brown, doubtless it was all for the best.

"Well," said Kate when she had digested the news, "so your Mr. Brown will have to think again, won't he? Perhaps at long last, he will decide to reap the benefits of his unsolicited philanthropy and invite you to share his hearth and home and be a comfort to his old age."

"Oh, do you really think so? It would, of course, be the natural way to repay himself for all his expense and trouble."

"No, I don't," Kate answered rather sharply. "If his thoughts were running in those channels he would have made his intentions clear long ago. You should have grown out of romantic fantasies of father-figures and star-crossed lovers awaiting rewards. For all you know, your Mr. Brown may be no one person, but a hard-headed syndicate of old cronies of your father's with a debt to pay. Have you thought of that?"

"Often. It's the most likely explanation, isn't it? Still, when one is growing up, it's important to have something or someone to fix one's sights on, and it was much more satisfying to invent images for Mr. Brown than to think of him just as a Trust," Victoria answered, and there was a touch of apology in Kate's smile.

"Yes, it must have been. Well, what are your own ideas in view of this latest development?"

"To find a job, obviously, and since poor Scottie's no longer available to make a home for me, Mr. Brown may have to revise his antediluvian ideas."

"Antediluvian?"

"Well, stuffy, anyway, considering the times and my situation. So far, any suggestions to become self-supporting haven't met with much success."

"And what would you like to do?"

Victoria twined one long, black-clad leg around the other and gazed out across the snowy slopes with that enquiring consideration which always intrigued Kate.

"Oh, impossible things, of course. Becoming a great ballerina, discovering a lost land, riding the winner of the National to victory — fantasies with the ignoble end in view of cocking snooks at Mr. Brown," she answered.

"In point of fact, I suppose my qualifications can't have a very high rating commercially, but there must be someone somewhere willing to employ me after such an expensive education."

Kate smiled without making any immediate comment, and sat turning over a half-formed project in her mind, then she said casually:

"Would you care to give the Allens a trial if it could be arranged?"

The girl's thin face became instantly so alive with naïve delight that for a moment Kate regretted having made an offer which might well be vetoed in other quarters.

"Work for you, Mrs. Allen?" Victoria exclaimed ecstatically. "But that would be pure heaven! What would I do? When could I start?"

"Gently, child, it's only a tentative suggestion to fill in time while you were looking around for something more suitable. You mightn't find life at Farthings such heaven after the advantages of being finished abroad. We live very quietly and don't entertain."

Victoria regarded her with grave, suddenly unchild-like eyes, the vivacity dying out of her face, leaving it blank and a little pinched.

"But don't you understand?" she said like an anxious child. "I'm grateful, of course, for what has been done for me, but I've never had any feeling of permanence. You treat me as a person, you see, and Farthings sounds like a real home."

"Yes," Kate answered with gentleness, "I think it has that quality. I only rent it, you know, but it's mine for as long as I need it."

"Need it? But won't you always need a home for Timmy?"

"Yes, of course, but one day he'll grow up and I won't want to be tied to one place for ever. In the meantime Farthings serves us very well, but there are domestic problems. Timmy needs companionship while I'm working and my old Elspeth who's been with us since he was born has enough to do with cooking and running the house to be at the beck and call of a child. He doesn't need a nanny now but someone young enough to play with him as well as teach him his alphabet. You and he seemed to click at once. Do you think you could be happy being a general dogsbody for a time?"

"I don't need to think. I can imagine nothing more— more rewarding than to share in your family life at Farthings for a little while. Oh, damn, there's Mr. Brown!"

For a moment Kate looked up, startled, half expecting to see an elderly stranger bearing down upon them, then she laughed.

"Don't cross your bridges. Just write to the solicitors and state your wishes. After all, you're nearly twenty and entitled to order your own life within reason," she said.

"Yes, I am, aren't I? But they don't treat me as an adult. They won't consider my wishes if they've got other plans."

"Well, you can but write and find out. I'm quite willing to present myself and my credentials for their inspection if necessary."

"Do you know any influential people — the sort, I

19

mean, to impress lawyers?" Victoria asked hopefully, and Kate laughed.

"One or two, I expect," she said. "The cousin from whom I rent my house would doubtless put in a word if asked, but you must put your own case first. After all, it's possible that your Mr. Brown is faced with a problem owing to this fresh development. You can hardly stop on here indefinitely now that your education is finished."

"Mr. Brown is never faced with problems, and if he was, Mr. Chapple or Mr. Ponsonby would devise means to iron them out with prompt dispatch. It's being borne in on me of late that they must have made a very good thing out of Mr. Brown's little ploy all these years," said Victoria astutely, and Kate's eyebrows went up.

"Very likely, but one must assume that rich eccentrics expect to pay for their whims, so run along and get that letter off before it's too late to alter plans."

CHAPTER TWO

BUT as the days went by with no reply to her letter, Victoria's spirits sank. At first she had consoled herself with the thought that negotiations would have to be effected with Mr. Brown who might well be at the other ends of the earth engaged on one of those nameless projects which Mr. Ponsonby had said covered such a wide field, but when, still without news, the day came for the Allens to leave for England, their departure seemed to put an end to her hopes.

"After all, it was only a dream," she said as she bade them goodbye, and Kate gave her a quick kiss.

"Cheer up! One's never sure what's round the corner, and for all you know, your Mr. Brown may be laid up with some dire complaint and unable to conduct any business," she said lightly, and was amused to see Victoria's face undergo one of its lightning transitions.

"I never thought of that!" she exclaimed. "Oh, poor Mr. Brown! And all this time I've been thinking unworthy things about him. I must write at once, and tell the lawyers not to worry him."

"I shouldn't bother," Kate retorted somewhat dryly. "I doubt if they would be impressed by a belated concern for their client. You have, I fancy, a secret fondness for this unknown patron, Victoria, or is it just wishful thinking?"

Victoria stood considering with that grave deliberation which she employed at times before answering the question.

"Perhaps," she said then. "Perhaps everyone needs a figurehead — a kind of touchstone against adversity. I hardly knew my father, you see, for I so seldom saw him. I admired him tremendously from a distance, but he wasn't much more real than Mr. Brown, so if ever I do meet Mr. Brown, I shall find something to like in him — even to love, if necessary."

"In that case content yourself with your own creations, the reality may turn out to be a big let-down," Kate retorted with some crispness, and as the sound of approaching sleighbells announced that the hour of departure was upon them, Victoria turned to her with a forlorn attempt to smile.

"Oh, I *shall* miss you—you and Timmy, and all the fun we've had. Perhaps it was a pity we met, after all."

"Nonsense, child! Even if you aren't allowed to accept employment with me we shall meet when you're back in England. You can at least come on a visit to Farthings and we'll pick up the threads again."

"That will be nice," Victoria replied politely but without conviction. Then Timmy created a timely diversion by clutching Victoria tightly round the legs and bursting into anguished wails.

"Don't want to go home . . . don't want to leave T—Toria . . . I won't, I won't, I *won't!*" he shouted, scarlet in the face, and by the time his mother and Victoria had soothed him into a hiccoughing state of compliance, there was no margin left for prolonged farewells.

Victoria picked up the bundle of English periodicals which Kate had left behind for her and sat down to idle away the time, reluctant to return to the hostel. Most of the glossies were filled with seasonable snapshots of notable winter sports enthusiasts holidaying at the more fahionable resorts. Under one of them a familiar name caught her eye and she read the caption: *Mr. Robert Farmer, who has recently added fresh laurels to his legal reputation, relaxing in the sun.* Mr. Robert Farmer was certainly relaxing with a glamorous blonde alongside, but since an enormous straw sombrero was tipped well over his face, he could have been anyone, thought Victoria, and upon picking up *Country Life,* was irritated to find that he figured here too. *Our candid camera catches Mr. Robert Farmer in holiday mood on the slopes at St. Moritz,* she was informed cosily. *A little bird whispers that this brilliant young junior Counsel might be thinking of settling down, so we may expect to hear an important announcement soon*. So he hadn't married after all, thought Victoria, hoping the little bird might still be a forerunner of disaster, at the same time examining the photograph for remembered characteristics, but here, too, Mr. Farmer was effectively disguised by a large pair of dark glasses. It was odd how the mention of him could still rankle, she reflected as she made her way back to the hostel, and was thankful that this modest little holiday resort was not smart enough to attract a more publicised clientele.

There was a postcard from Kate at the end of the week announcing their safe arrival, but nothing from Chapple, Chapple & Ponsonby, and Victoria sat down to pen a tactful reminder that she was still awaiting instructions and were they aware that the hostel would shortly be closing down for its spring respite before the start of the climbing season?

When at last the reply came, she opened it with no anticipation of agreement, but whether her arguments had at last found favour, or whether Kate's efforts had proved more persuasive and her credentials suitably impressive, permission was granted for a trial run agreed upon with Mrs. Allen on certain terms. There followed precise instructions as to dates of departure and modes of travel and concluded with prim good wishes for the future.

From then on the days seemed to fly past and all too soon she was making her farewells and discovering with some surprise that she would be missed. For a moment as her plane took off from the airport, she experienced regret for those carefree months which would never come again and could be grateful now for that meticulous attention to her father's wishes which at the time had seemed so pointless. Later as the plane passed over the English coast and touched down on English soil, such philosophic musings vanished on a wave of eager anticipation. She was a child again, returning for the holidays, but this time it was a real homecoming. There was Kate waiting at the barrier and signalling frantically and all around her was the almost forgotten buzz of English voices and the inevitable patter and hissing of English rain.

"Oh, *Kate*! If it wasn't so wet and dirty, I'd fall on my knees and kiss the ground like what's-his-name," she cried as she was clasped in a warm embrace, then grew pink with embarrassment. "Oh, how *awful*! I've never called you that before, and now you're my employer! It was just that I was so pleased to see you that I didn't think."

"Well, please go on forgetting," Kate replied, her brown eyes twinkling. "I hope we're going to be friends rather than mistress and mother's help, for which neither of us are very well fitted. Come along now—we've got a fair drive ahead of us and it's a stinking day."

It was, indeed, a most unpleasant day, but to Victoria, repeatedly rubbing a clear spot in the condensation on the passenger window and peering out at familiar surroundings, it seemed only right that the weather should be traditional on her return to her native land.

"How did you work it? Did you blackmail old Mr. Chapple? Did you even, perhaps, get into the Presence and do a spot of persuasion on Mr. Brown?" she asked among other less relevant questions, and Kate laughed.

"No, I did *not* get into the Presence—it didn't occur to me to try," she replied. "As it happens, Chapple, Chapple & Ponsonby handled my affairs when my husband died, so I wasn't unknown to them."

Kate turned her attention again to the countryside. New estates and factory sites seemed to have encroached still further on green fields and commons, but gradually these were left behind and the car took a sudden plunge down a steep, winding hill into the narrow lanes and wooded pockets of the Sussex Weald. Every so often a gap in the trees would reveal an unbroken vista of rolling country, but the line of downs lying beyond was hidden in a misty curtain of rain. Another hill was climbed, twisting sharply through the trees, and at the top Kate turned the car into a rough, puddle-pitted lane which ended at a pair of white gates standing open to the long, mellow walls of an old farmhouse.

Even in the rainy bleakness of a March afternoon,

Farthings offered a welcome and a sense of homecoming and Victoria fell in love with it on sight. Kate gave her no time to stand and stare, however, but hustled her in out of the wet, and there was Timmy clutching her round the legs with the remembered tenacity, though this time his fervour found expression in piercing squeals of delight.

"You've come for always, haven't you, Toria? Elpet *said* it was just to visit, but it *isn't*, is it?" he said as she hugged him in return.

"Now, young man, don't plague the young leddy as soon as she's set foot through the door," said a big, capable-looking woman hurrying to relieve them of their luggage. "Losh me, Mrs. Allen, don't you go out in the wet again. Sam will fetch in the rest of your traps and put the car away, too."

"Very well," Kate smiled. "Victoria, this is my dear Elspeth of whom you've often heard me speak. She manages the house and us with equal impartiality. I expect she'll manage you, too, if you don't make a stand from the start. Elspeth, this is Miss Hayes who is going to take Timmy off your hands for a bit and think up fresh uses for magic for me when I run out of plots."

"How do you do?" Victoria said, disentangling herself from Timmy and holding out a hand.

Elspeth took it after an instant's deliberation and Victoria, watching the woman's shrewd grey eyes travelling over her face, knew that she was being silently appraised.

"We're pleased to welcome you here to Farthings, miss," she said politely, but there was reserve behind the pleasant burr of her native Scotland and Victoria knew that Elspeth would accept her only when she had formed her own assessment.

"Well," said Kate, hoping that her old servant would not extend her past distrust of the au pair girls to Victoria, "I expect you'd like to see your room and freshen up generally, after which we'll have our well-earned tea. I know Elspeth was making a batch of her special griddle scones in your honour, so come along and I'll show you the lie of the land."

Very soon it seemed to Victoria that she had known Farthings all her life, or perhaps, as Kate pointed out, it was simply her first real experience of home.

Mr. Brown was forgotten for days on end in the pleasure of fresh discoveries. She loved the old rambling house with its many passages and hidden stairways and rooms opening invitingly one upon another. Elspeth grumbled at the inconvenience when it came to carrying coals and trays, but she kept the place spotless with only the help of a daily girl from the village and a youth who periodically dug the garden and cleaned the car, and would allow no one but herself to wax and polish the rather fine period pieces which graced many of the rooms. It was a long time before Victoria realised that the contents of the house which seemed so much to reflect Kate's tastes belonged to her no more than the house itself.

"Took the whole lot furnished at a nominal rent for these times and no strings attached," Elspeth told her. "It was a merciful dispensation at the time of her trouble, for poor Mr. Allen left very little money and the bairn needed special care and quiet, born as he was. Aye, there's some good folks in this world yet."

Victoria remembered that Kate had said she leased Farthings from a cousin for as long as she might need it. She must be a very nice and devoted cousin, Victoria thought, to offer her home for an indefinite period, unless for some reason she had never cared for it herself.

"Yes," she said, "that was generous of the cousin, but perhaps she's old, or maybe lives abroad?"

Elspeth paused in her attentions to a piecrust table long enough to favour Victoria with a look of amused surprise, then fell to again with renewed vigour.

"Neither old nor female, and as far as I know has no thoughts of settling abroad," she retorted.

"Oh, I see. I suppose I took the sex for granted because this house has a sort of family feeling, if you know what I mean."

26

"Aye, I ken what you mean, but the leddy didn't share your views, it seems."

"What lady?" Elspeth so often had the trick of presupposing you could follow her line of thought.

"The leddy who should have come here as a bride, of course. The poor gentleman couldna be expected to fancy the place on his own, so Mrs. Allen keeps it warm for him. Now will you leave me to get on with my redding, Miss Toria? The bairn won't hurt in the woods this fine morn, but mind that weak leg of his on rough ground."

Victoria could hear Kate tapping away on her typewriter as she passed the study on her way to the nursery, and wondered vaguely what sort of person the male cousin might be; elderly, one might suppose, and contemplating a second marriage, since Farthings and its contents had all the familiar hallmarks of a previous home. The nameless lady of his choice must have been hard to please if she could resist the charms of such a place, Victoria reflected, then felt a rather guilty sense of thankfulness for the timely misfortune of another.

March had slipped into April. The banks were starred with primroses and the woods with the first leafy freshness of spring and in the little orchard the tight pink buds on the apple trees were ready to burst into blossom.

One morning when Victoria was helping Elspeth in the kitchen, they heard a car stop at the gates, followed by Timmy's delighted squeals of recognition.

"Now, who would that be just when lunch is ready to go on the table?" Elspeth exclaimed with annoyance. "If it's a body dropping in expecting a meal there'll no be enough to go round. The butcher brought three chops the morn instead of the wee joint I ordered."

"It's probably Dr. Squires fitting us in between calls," Victoria said. Kate had few visitors, but the doctor frequently dropped in to keep a professional eye on Timmy, although Victoria suspected that he had rather more than a passing regard for Kate.

"Aye, very likely. Well, he'll be no trouble. Bread and cheese and a dram is all he'll have time for, no doubt.

27

Run and tell Mrs. Allen, she'll not be taking any heed if she's stuck in the middle of a chapter."

But Kate was already hurrying across the hall, holding out welcoming hands with much less restraint than she accorded the doctor, and the tall man who stepped over the threshold with Timmy tugging violently at his trouser leg took her hands in his and kissed her affectionately.

"*Rob!*" she cried with surprised delight as he released her. "Why on earth didn't you let me know? It's been such an age that I thought you must have forgotten us."

"That's blatant fishing, as well you know," he replied. "I've been snowed under lately or I'd have cadged a week-end before now. Can you do with me at such short notice? I hadn't time to do more than fling a few things together and hop into the car."

` "Of course we can do with you. Your old room's always ready and we only have to make up the bed. Timmy, for goodness' sake stop tugging at Uncle Rob's trousers — there won't be any crease left!" Kate laughed, then became aware of Victoria waiting a little uncertainly to be introduced. "Oh, I'm forgetting my manners in the un-expectedness of the moment. This is Timmy's Toria who has nearly cut you out, so you'll have to be very tactful if you want to share his affections."

Victoria came forward to shake hands. There had been something vaguely familiar about the stranger's voice, but the light had been behind him so that his features were indistinct. When he turned to acknowledge the introduction however, and she encountered a pair of cool, appraising eyes under hair that was dark when it should have been grey, she experienced an unwelcome shock of recognition. When she had last seen him he had been grey, the grey of a wig pushed carelessly back from his forehead matching the grey of his cold, fastidious regard. The memories of that bewildering day in court had faded like the recollections of a nightmare, but Mr. Robert Farmer had never been forgotten and, for a moment, old impressions renewed themselves so vividly that she found herself stammering when she responded with conventional greetings and knew the colour had risen in her cheeks.

He shook hands, making some mock-rueful reference to Timmy's vacillating affections, but there was no recognition in his eyes and after a moment of incurious attention he turned back to Kate with whom he was clearly on excellent terms.

"Darling, run and tell Elspeth that my cousin is here, will you?" Kate said to Victoria. "She'll be very angry with you, Robert, for not giving her a chance to provide your favourite lunch, but I expect you'll get round her as you always do. Now come along into the parlour for a glass of sherry and tell me all you've been doing since last we met."

Victoria thought it tactful to leave them to themselves until luncheon was ready and stayed in the kitchen admiring the resource with which Elspeth contrived to make a substantial meal from the meagre rations of the butcher's chops. All the time she chattered reminiscently about Mr. Rab, who was plainly a favourite, and Victoria learnt with growing surprise that he was the self-same cousin from whom Kate rented the house.

"Then it was Mr. Farmer's bride who wouldn't live here, was it?" she asked.

"Aye. A fashionable besom with a taste for parties and fine clothes, so I'm told. She ran off with one of those pop singers and divorced him within the year, it's said."

"Oh!" said Victoria, wondering how much the jilted Mr. Farmer had minded. "Has he married someone else?"

"If he had, Mrs. Allen would hardly be living here, would she?" Elspeth retorted with a certain asperity. "I'd like to think—still, it's no my business, nor yet yours, so I'll be obliged if you'll carry in the vegetables for me, Miss Toria, and then tell them lunch is ready."

By the time she sat down with them at table, Victoria had recovered her self-possession, rather enjoying the knowledge that she had the advantage of Mr. Robert Farmer in the matter of acquaintance. It was hardly surprising, of course, that he had failed to recognise an unremarkable schoolgirl who, save for provoking him to a fine display of fireworks, could have made little impression as an individual out of the scores of witnesses which must be his daily lot. She had to admit that off duty he possess-ed a degree of easy charm which found a ready response in Kate and, remembering Elspeth's unfinished remark in the kitchen, wondered if there might be more to a bene-volent concession in the matter of his house than cousinly kindness.

"You've been exceptionally silent, darling," Kate ob-served as they left the dining-room, "still, I'm afraid we've rather been holding the floor. You and Robert must get acquainted, for you'll be seeing plenty of each other if we can persuade him to come down more often. You can't think, Rob, how nice it is to have a man about the house again."

"Has the good doctor given up calling, then?" he asked with a faint twinkle, and she made a face at him.

"Certainly not. He's most attentive to Timmy's needs," she replied primly. "But poor Victoria has little chance to show off the finished results of her expensive education. There aren't many eligible young men in these parts and if there were her rather stuffy guardians would probably dis-approve."

"Guardians?"

"One, to be precise, and he isn't really a guardian at all. Victoria, take Robert round the garden and tell him about your mysterious Mr. Brown while I finish correcting those proofs. I really must try to get them off by the afternoon post."

Victoria, not relishing the prospect of a tête-à-tête with the stranger until she had decided on her line of conduct, made hurried excuses, but Kate said nonsense to all of them and went away to her study, and Victoria, catching Mr. Robert Farmer's eye resting upon her with somewhat sardonic amusement, knew that he was fully aware of her reluctance and rather enjoying himself.

"Are you shy, Timmy's Toria?" he enquired a little mockingly, and now that they were alone together, her old antagonism revived.

"Certainly not," she replied, endeavouring to sound cool and assured. "At my Paris establishment we were taught that it was impolite to appear gauche whatever our provocation."

"Very proper, but weren't you taught that it was also impolite to leave a guest to his own devices?"

"Of course, but you're Kate's guest, not mine, and since you're related and this house is yours, I didn't suppose that you needed entertaining."

"Touché. Still, if I were to ask you very politely if you would be so kind as to take me round the garden, perhaps you would stifle your disinclination and oblige?"

"Certainly, Mr. Farmer, if that's what you want," she said at once. "We'll find Timmy and take him with us."

"I've always understood that Timmy rested at this hour, but perhaps you've instituted a new regime," he said, and Victoria could have kicked herself. She had quite genuinely forgotten that Timmy would not be available for another hour, but in saying the first thing that came into her head, she could only have confirmed whatever he was probably thinking.

"Of course, I'd forgotten. We have so few visitors here, you see, that your sudden arrival has rather thrown out our routine." It was a feeble enough explanation and had a distinctly governessy flavour, she thought crossly, then saw him grin with a most unexpected touch of mischief and found herself grinning back.

"That's better," he said, taking her by the arm and piloting her out into the garden. "You shouldn't try conclusions with me on such short acquaintance, you know. I have quite a reputation for dealing firmly with evasive witnesses."

"So I believe," she replied rather tartly. "It must be very uplifting to the ego to browbeat witnesses who can't answer back."

"Oh, but some of them do, and I only browbeat the stubborn ones. Tell me about your mysterious Mr. Brown. Is he an admirer?"

Victoria was not given to inventing fantasies to boost her own consequence, but Robert Farmer seemed to have the knack of making her feel a child again. It would do him no harm to keep him guessing.

31

"Mr. Brown . . ." she repeated musingly. "Now, there's a man who thoroughly understands the romantic approach."

"By being mysterious?"

"That and other things."

"What other things?"

"You're very inquisitive, aren't you, Mr. Farmer, considering we've only just met."

They were strolling through the little orchard which bounded the neat approach to Farthings. Here nature had been left to run wild and the grass was already ankle deep. The fruit trees were long past bearing, but they still put forth blossom and Victoria paused now to reach up to a low-hanging branch and shake the last of the petals about her. Robert stood and watched her with obliging attention, thinking that she was probably quite aware of the charming picture she presented, then she laughed as a shower of dew fell on her upturned face and opened her mouth like a child to catch the drops.

"Very pretty," he observed with a certain dryness. "No doubt the romantic Mr. Brown would immediately respond in the appropriate manner were he here to observe."

She looked at him with a moment's surprised enquiry as if she had temporarily forgotten him, then she let the branch spring back with a final shower of dew and blossom and stood trying to shake the petals out of her long hair.

"Allow me," Robert said, and neatly removed those that clung more tenaciously.

"I never said he was romantic," she protested while she stood passively under his ministrations.

"No? Well, I certainly thought that was implied. A man who thoroughly understands the romantic approach should have all the right answers. Is he romantic-looking too, this paragon?"

"I don't know."

"You don't *know?*"

"I've never seen him," Victoria snapped, wishing that she had not embarked on such an unrewarding line of evasion.

"Dear me! Does he appear masked?" Robert absently tucked a piece of hair behind her ear as he spoke and she shook her head impatiently to free it.

"Of course he doesn't. Don't do that, please. I like to keep my ears covered."

"Why? Do you suffer from earache?"

"You are the most aggravating person I've ever met and ask far too many questions," she replied, exasperated both with him and with herself. "No, I do *not* suffer from earache, but my ears are my worst feature, if you must know, and I've been taught to hide them."

"*Are* they? Let me look again." He restrained her with a gentle hand before she could break away from him and swept her hair to one side to inspect her ears with earnest attention.

"H'm . . . a trifle large, possibly, by fashionable standards, but they are most engagingly pointed, rather like a faun's. Perhaps you're a changeling."

She ducked under his arm and backed away from him, her eyes bright with anger.

"Well, now that you've had your fun at my expense, Mr. Farmer, perhaps you'll consider yourself sufficiently entertained for one afternoon and allow me to get on with the chores for which I'm paid," she said.

"Now that," he retorted with infuriating good humour, "is a splendid exit line. Puts me in my place and reminds me of yours with admirable restraint. Still, you will admit that you've had your bit of fun, too."

"What do you mean? I was only following Kate's instructions and trying to amuse the guest."

"With some success, though possibly not as you intended. I have a longer memory than you give me credit for."

"What do you mean?" she said again, but with less assurance. "I'm a stranger to you."

"No, no, Miss Victoria Mary Hayes, I recognised you at once. I hasten to add that the transformation since last we met is quite charming, but I couldn't be mistaken in those ears," said Robert Farmer and, turning on his heel, strolled back to the house.

CHAPTER THREE

"YOU might have warned me," Victoria said to Kate after Robert had returned to London.

"Warned you of what?"

"That the cousin who owns this house was Mr. Farmer."

"I'm afraid it never occurred to me that you would be interested."

"But you must have known he was involved in my father's case."

Kate's eyes rested on her thoughtfully for a moment and her eyebrows rose a fraction.

"Yes, of course I knew, but you were a child at the time, and I didn't suppose you'd even remember him."

"Not remember! It's true I was too young to understand the rights and wrongs of the affair, but Mr. Robert Farmer I've not forgotten. He made a nonsense of my evidence and enjoyed every minute of it."

"Dear me!" said Kate mildly. "I'd no idea you still cherished a grievance. I can understand that the experience must have been bewildering and alarming, but you must surely realise now that there was nothing personal in Robert's methods of cross-examination and the only enjoyment he would derive would be the satisfaction in establishing and winning his case. You've never mentioned him before Victoria, and I didn't suppose you'd even remember his name."

"I used, when I was younger," said Victoria reminiscently, "to make up splendid stories of dire retribution overtaking Mr. Farmer. Like Mr. Brown, he stuck in my mind, but for rather different reasons." She spoke with an effort to minimise any suggestion that Kate had been remiss, by admitting to childish fantasies as if they were well behind her, but for once Kate did not respond with her usual amused tolerance.

"It's to be hoped then that you're adult enough by now to have grown out of such pastimes," she said a little sharply. "Mr. Brown, I suppose, is fair game since he chooses to pander to your fancies by remaining invisible, but Robert is a different kettle of fish and I'm very fond of him. I'm sorry that you evidently can't bring yourself to think more kindly of him, since he will be coming down here quite often, I hope, but you can always keep out of his way."

"I'm sorry," Victoria apologised. "I didn't mean to be personal in any way. It was so unexpected meeting him again and finding you were both related that it threw me a little. I hope I wasn't rude."

"Oh, no, just a little prickly and on your dignity. It's a sure way to bring out the worst in Robert, let me warn you, so if you don't want him to tease, stop trailing your coat."

"Do I do that?"

"Well, perhaps not consciously, but Robert's a bad person to tangle with when it comes to disagreement, as you must have discovered years ago, so be careful." Kate spoke with a return of her old affectionate lightness and Victoria wondered if she had imagined that touch of resentment earlier, but she remembered Kate's pleasure in the week-end and Elspeth's unspoken approval and thought more humbly of her own objections. Since she was fond of Kate and knew something of her earlier tragedy she could not feel that a man as cold and sharp-tongued as Robert Farmer was right for her, but if Kate's inclinations lay in that direction, then the least she could do was to accept his occasional presence at Farthings with a good grace.

It was not so easy, however, to remain impartially in the background. Robert, whose last-minute descents upon them became more frequent as summer approached, showed a perverse liking for her company when Kate was not available, and although she did not flatter herself that his casual attentions were inspired by anything other than a desire to provoke her into argument for the pleasure of proving her wrong, she found herself having unexpected moments of doubt when he chose, instead, to charm her.

"Why are you so quick to take my harmless pleasantries

35

amiss?" he asked her once, and was intrigued as Kate so often was by her grave deliberation before replying.

"Possibly because I'm never sure that your pleasantries *are* harmless, Mr. Farmer," she said then, and his eyebrows lifted.

"Dear me! I don't seem to be making much headway, do I? And can't you bring yourself to address me less formally?" he said, and she twisted round on the garden bench to regard him with more indifference than she felt.

"I will call you Robert if you prefer it," she answered with rather prim composure, "but I hardly think that you would concern yourself over making headway or not."

"Wouldn't you? But then you don't know me very well, do you?"

"Well enough. You forget I've already had a taste of your humours in court."

They had been sunning themselves on the sheltered patio behind the house waiting for Kate to summon them in for tea and without any warning his fingers closed on her shoulder in a none too gentle grip.

"The taste you had then, my child, was mild compared to what you would get now," he retorted, and the lazy banter had gone from his voice. "I would advise you to think twice before trying to get your own back with childish attempts to sting me. My sting can be a deal more deadly than yours, so don't tempt fate."

"Do you keep your sting in your tail, like the scorpion, Mr. Farmer?" she said, unable to resist retaliating even while she knew she was no match for him.

"That you will doubtless find out in due course, Miss Hayes," he replied, mocking her, but with an underlying note of warning, and Victoria was relieved when Kate appeared to announce that tea was ready.

As always when Kate was present, the tempo changed to a pleasant impression of family unity. Victoria could forget her easily aroused hostility, listening to their warm exchanges and watching Robert's ease and patience with the little boy. Timmy plainly adored him and sometimes she would catch Kate looking at her son and her cousin with a rueful expression as if she were regretting some un-explained decision in the past.

"Robert's very fond of Timmy, isn't he?" she said to Kate when they were alone again.

"Well, he's Timmy's godfather, so I suppose there's a special bond," Kate answered tranquilly. "Timmy, of course, is too young to miss a father he never knew and Robert makes a very good stand-in."

"Would you marry again, Kate?" Victoria asked, re-membering Elspeth's hints, but Kate, if she was aware of the obvious train of thought, avoided any direct admission.

"I don't know," she answered placidly. "Timmy will need a father when he's grown beyond my capabilities, but marriage embraces more than that."

Victoria's eyes were at once apologetic. "Yes, of course. And when one has loved very much once, it wouldn't, I imagine, be easy to put up with second best."

Kate glanced at her with amusement. "Easier than you think, my dear. Compromise isn't such a bad thing if you look it squarely in the face. Jim—my husband—and I were very happy during the short time we had together, but I was in love with someone else when I married him. Don't look so shocked, Victoria, the world isn't really well lost for love, you know, and it's silly to go crying for the moon when a lesser light will suit very well."

Victoria said nothing while she tried to readjust her ideas. She had taken for granted that Kate's marriage had been a love-match, and she was still young enough to feel cheated out of a romantic ending.

"This other man—why didn't you marry him?" she asked. "Had he got a wife already?"

"No, but he was engaged to somebody else, and I've never believed much happiness would come from break-ing up a love affair."

"So you married your Jim to make things final. No going back."

"There's never any going back whatever you may decide."

"Isn't there? No second chances? No opportunities to begin again?"

37

"Well, that might depend on circumstances, I suppose. I doubt, in my own case, whether my decision made much difference except to me, as the other engagement came to nothing."

"What a waste of noble intentions! If only you'd waited, Kate!" Victoria sounded so outraged that Kate had to laugh.

"Nothing of the kind," she retorted with some briskness. "I was never very good at waiting and Jim made me an excellent husband. I've never had regrets, so don't go investing me with a tragic past to lend colour to those imageries of yours. Stick to your creations for Mr. Brown which will never give you cause for disillusionment, since it seems unlikely that you will meet him in the flesh."

"But I will one day," Victoria said softly, diverted as Kate had intended back to her own affairs. "In fifteen months the Trust will be wound up and I'll be responsible to no one for my bed and board. He can hardly refuse a meeting then to round things off — besides, however old or busy he may be, he must surely have some spark of natural curiosity as to how his human experiment has turned out."

"Well, time will show," said Kate, refusing as usual to commit herself, "but don't build too much on conventional happy endings. I fancy your Mr. Brown is not over-much concerned with the human angle or he would have made himself known before now."

"Yes, I suppose you're right, but I shall track him down somehow. Apart from anything else, I couldn't bear to spend the rest of my life with my own curiosity unsatisfied," Victoria said, and although she would have liked to return to the more present subject of Kate's affairs, she had too much sensibility to probe.

They did not see much of Robert for some time, for the courts kept him busy and an ever-growing practice made demands which Kate said put an unnecessary strain on a man who could well afford to turn down briefs.

"Well, I suppose he needs the money. It must take quite a packet to pay for all those expensive aids to gracious living," Victoria said, and Kate gave her a sidelong look.

"You sound censorious," she said mildly. "There's nothing pretentious about Robert's mode of living. He just has a taste for quality and since he can afford the best he naturally sees that he gets it."

Victoria glanced across at her in surprise, imagining a touch of resentment in her reply.

"I didn't mean to be. I was only countering your suggestion that he could afford to turn down briefs," she said.

"Well, so he can. He inherited quite a sizeable fortune from his father who made money in oil and could pick and choose without running himself ragged."

Victoria's eyes widened. It was true that such indications of Robert's well-lined pockets were sober and unobtrusive, but she had rubbed shoulders too long with Madame's richer pupils not to appreciate the cost of such niceties.

"Perhaps he can't resist living up to his reputation and keeping in the public eye," she suggested without any intention of sounding critical, but Kate frowned.

"I wish you liked Robert better," she said. "His manner can be misleading, but he's a tender-hearted creature at bottom. He's been a very good friend to Timmy and me."

"Yes, I know."

"He should have married, of course, but he took that business of Irene pretty hard. Apart from throwing his affections back in his face she made a laughing stock of him running off with that frightful pop heart-throb, and Robert's a proud man. It's partly the reason he works so unnecessarily hard, I often think. Stops you from brooding at first and then becomes a habit."

"Kate—have you ever thought—" Victoria began impulsively, but checked herself as she caught Kate's cool glance. Friendship had ripened pleasantly between them during the past weeks, but Kate was rarely addicted to confidences.

"I've thought a lot of things too trivial to be of value," she said, neatly evading a direct answer, "but one thing I *can* tell you without betraying any promises, which might

39

make you feel more kindly towards Robert. You primarily have him to thank for being here."

"What on earth can you mean, Kate? We met by chance in Gruse and it was chance again that Robert turned out to be a connecting link."

"Not entirely. He knew I might run across you in such a small place and suggested you might be suitable for Timmy. I was to form my own judgment and act accordingly."

"But how on earth could he know I was there?"

"He presumably made enquiries. Chapple & Ponsonby have put work in his way from time to time and he's on good terms with the old gentleman. Don't you remember I told you at the time I had a cousin who might put in a good word should your Mr. Brown prove difficult?"

"Yes, I do, but I never dreamed—and I thought the cousin was a woman, anyway. How very odd that he should have remembered all this time."

"Not really. I told you Robert has an unsuspected soft centre and he was upset by the case at the time. No one could foresee that your father would take the way out that he did, but it left a nasty taste, all mixed up with the mess of Robert's own affairs."

Victoria was silent. It was surprising to learn Robert must have kept track of her from time to time, and for the first time, she began to think of him as a human being who could be subject to hurt like any other.

"Well," said Kate who had been watching her swift changes of expression with interest, "have I succeeded in getting you to have second thoughts?"

"Second thoughts?"

"More adult ones, shall we say, than those you've cherished since the age of fourteen."

"Yes, it *was* childish. I suppose, comforting myself with imaginary scenes of dire retribution was as silly as inventing impossible images for Mr. Brown," Victoria said, trying to laugh at her fancies, and Kate smiled.

"Mr. Brown was a natural in view of the circumstances, but I wonder why Robert stuck in your mind with equal vividness," she observed a little dryly, and Victoria frowned.

"I suppose because he made a deep impression on me at a time when everything familiar seemed suddenly to be swept away," she said slowly. "There has to be a villian in all self-respecting fairy-tales, as you should know, and Mr. Robert Farmer filled the part to a T."

"While Mr. Fairy-godfather Brown reigned smug and aloof on his pedestal."

"Yes, perhaps he is a bit smug," agreed Victoria seriously, "but I expect you get that way if you dwell upon Olympus."

"Very likely. Well, at least you can absolve Robert of that. He may be provocative, and often infuriating, but he's never smug," Kate said, and Victoria asked a little tentatively:

"Why are you trying so hard to convince me, Kate? It can't really matter to Robert whether I like him or not."

"I daresay it doesn't, but it matters to me. I like harmony in the home and since Farthings belongs to Robert he's entitled to treat it as such."

"Yes, of course, I keep forgetting. Farthings doesn't seem at all the sort of place an oil magnate would have chosen to settle down in."

"Neither did he. Old man Farmer had a taste for roving, I understand, and seldom saw his son. Farthings belonged to an aunt of Robert's who used to have him for the school holidays. She was a maiden lady with no family ties and left it to him when she died together with all the treasures she had collected over the years."

"And he's never lived here?"

"Only as a boy for holidays. Of course he intended settling here when he married and using the town flat as a convenience for work, but Irene had other ideas. She insisted on a house in London and wanted Robert to sell Farthings and buy a place in some fashionable resort where she could entertain her weekend guests with a nice display of chic. Such a silly thing to quarrel about."

"And Robert wouldn't?"

41

"No. He didn't insist that they lived here if Irene didn't care for it, but he wouldn't agree to selling. There was no reason why Irene should have made an issue of it except that she was vain and spoilt and had always had her own way. But she did, and when threats and recriminations failed to move him she upped and ran off with this frightful young man and lived to regret it, I'm glad to say."

"So you ill-wished her," Victoria said, and Kate looked quite startled.

"Yes, perhaps I did," she admitted ruefully. "Does that exonerate your own revengeful thoughts?"

"No, but it makes me feel less foolish for having had them. She can't have cared for him very much, can she, to demand her pound of flesh just to gratify a whim?"

"I don't think Irene would ever care for anyone as much as herself, but she was quite proud of having hooked Robert who was much sought after and never doubted she could twist him round her little finger."

"But the perspicacious Mr. Farmer so adept at putting his finger on any flaw in evidence — shouldn't he have seen through her?"

"Still not allowing poor Robert any human weaknesses? When a man as heartwhole as Robert becomes emotionally involved for the first time he's no wiser or less vulnerable than the rest of us, and Irene was very lovely."

"So he let you have Farthings instead," Victoria said, her first suspicions returning. "Perhaps it's the case of an ill wind."

"Perhaps it is, but that's another story," Kate replied rather sharply, and got up to lean out of a window to call to her son playing with his bricks on the lawn. It was a definite intimation that confidences were at an end and Victoria was too wise to persist, but she wondered again if Kate, so calm and well adjusted, was biding her time until Robert should come to share her view that compromise was no bad substitute for the unattainable. But what of Robert, so deep in love once, it seemed, that he could scarcely have been aware of another woman's feelings for him? Could he ever recapture what he had felt for Irene, or would he just be content with second-best and a wife who would not expect too much of him?

When Robert next came down he was tired and over-worked following a gruelling session in the courts and spent most of his time stretched out on one of Kate's lilos in a sunny corner of the patio. Perhaps, Victoria thought, she was looking at him with new eyes as a result of Kate's disclosures, but she found herself experiencing a most un-familiar desire to afford him small attentions, even to dis-persing the headache, which she was sure caused that little frown of discomfort, by smoothing it away as she did for Timmy after a bout of crying. She restrained herself, how-ever, from such an uncharacteristic offer which would surely be received with derisive comment, but Kate watch-ed her with amusement, gratified to note that the silly child had evidently profited by her casual hints. She hoped Robert would not nip a better relationship in the bud by administering one of his set-downs, but although he caught her eye with a quizzical glance from time to time, he forbore to tease.

When she left them, however, to plan the evening meal with Elspeth, he opened his eyes and enquired lazily:

"What's come over you, Victoria Mary Hayes? Do I imagine a brief cessation of hostilities or have you just run out of ammunition?"

"You won't provoke me, Robert, not today when the sun shines and you're enjoying a hard-earned rest," she countered, smiling at him while she mentally decided that she rather liked his cold, clever features in repose.

"Won't I? How disappointing. You rise so beautifully when you think I'm laughing at you."

"But half the time you are, aren't you?"

"Only with amused affection."

"Affection?"

"Don't sound so incredulous—I'm not entirely devoid of the more tender emotions." He spoke with a tinge of the old mockery, but she did not counter with her usual scorn.

"Perhaps I haven't had a chance to know you as you

43

really are. It's awfully easy to take people at face value, isn't it?" she said with an unfamiliar touch of shyness, and his face immediately resumed its mask of hardness.

"Am I to gather Kate has been talking?" he asked with a touch of distaste.

"Well, I think she thought I had the wrong idea of you. She only told me very briefly about that old affair—just to prove how wrong one's judgment could be. Kate's very fond of you, you know."

"Yes, Miss Prim, I do know, and don't let undigested notions run away with you. You're a little young to be sitting in judgment on your elders and betters, anyway," he retorted with a decided bite to his voice, but although she coloured a little, she smiled back at him with a serene refusal to be snubbed.

"I won't be put in my place by that old cliché. Perhaps you haven't realised I'll be twenty next week. In another year even Mr. Brown will have to acknowledge my adult status," she said, and he smiled back at her a shade wryly.

"Touché," he murmured, raising a hand to sketch a vague salute. "What a pity we invariably have to come back to the egregious Mr. Brown as arbiter."

"Well, he is for the time being, but why should you care?"

"I can't say I do very much, but I find his recurrence as a theme somewhat tedious."

"Well, he's a theme I've grown so accustomed to that I shall quite miss him when he disappears from the background," Victoria said, sounding both regretful and a little surprised, and Robert gave her a sharp glance.

"I believe you will. Well, I suppose there's something to be said for a nameless deity who supplies one with security without any obligation," he observed with some dryness, and she looked slightly shocked.

"Oh, but I have obligations and, even if I didn't get a sharp reminder when I'm remiss in reporting progress, I should feel a personal responsibility towards him," she said quickly. "I hope, when the time comes, he'll come out of hiding and let me thank him properly."

"Aha!" he exclaimed triumphantly. "I believe, despite

the lack of evidence, that you've been fostering romantic notions all along. Mr. Brown is the Frog Prince, or Beauty's Beast who will claim his reward in the usual way and suffer disenchantment for his pains."

"What *are* you talking about? I'll admit at first I had rosy hopes of getting adopted and becoming an old man's darling, but I never went further than that!"

"Didn't you, now? Well, there's yet time for a re-shuffle. Since, as you have pointed out, you've already reached the years of discretion, adoption must have gone by the board, but there's still the other alternative. What would you say if you found that marriage had been the end product in mind all along?"

"It would depend entirely on whether I found him acceptable or not," Victoria answered with engaging prim-ness, and he laughed.

"But you might consider it—as a token repayment for benefits received, shall we say?"

"Oh, you're being absurd! Whoever he may be, he'd scarcely cherish dreams of marrying a complete stranger seen only once as an unprepossessing schoolgirl!"

"Well, by the laws of average you will marry some worthy young man, and solve both your own and your unknown benefactor's problems," Robert said, raising his long body from its recumbent position with an im-patient jerk and getting to his feet.

"How cross you sound, suddenly," she said, her eyes on his elongated shadow stretching across the paving stones as he stood looking down at her. "You don't know me at all well, really, do you? No better than Mr. Brown does."

"Be damned to Mr. Brown! Can't we have any discussion without coming back to him?" Robert snapped, and reach-ing down a hand, pulled her smartly to her feet. It was the first time he had ever touched her and, perhaps because their recent exchanges had been devoid of that more usual undercurrent of hostility, she became aware of him in an entirely different dimension.

"No, you don't," Robert said, anticipating flight, and his fingers tightened on her shoulders. But she had made no attempt to break away, and stood there passively with her face uplifted. "After all, you're full of surprises, as befits a true daughter of Eve," he murmured with unexpected tenderness, and bent his dark head to kiss her with gentle insistence.

The sun was already gone from the patio leaving behind a sudden coolness to remind them that summer had not yet come and Kate's voice from the doorway had a matching crispness.

"You'd better come in now, both of you, it's getting chilly," she said, and Victoria slipped a little awkwardly from Robert's grasp and began picking up the scattered cushions.

"Dear Kate, do I detect a note of disapproval in your untimely summons?" Robert asked on a teasing note which held no embarrassment.

"Not at all. Perhaps I should have coughed discreetly in the best tradition," she replied lightly, but she did not smile and Victoria, standing irresolutely with the pile of gaily coloured cushions clasped to her chest, remembered too late her own suspicions regarding Kate's feelings.

"Can I do anything to help Elspeth?" she asked rather hurriedly.

"No. She won't thank you for getting under her feet when she's preparing a meal, but you might go up to Timmy and treat him to an extra bedtime story. He's been feeling a bit neglected," Kate said. "Robert, you're looking very tired. Come in and have a whisky and soda to warm you up before supper. I've lighted a fire in the parlour."

Victoria went upstairs and Robert followed his cousin into the small, charmingly panelled room which was used by Kate when she was alone in preference to the larger drawing-room and still retained the old-fashioned name it had been known by in Miss Eva Farmer's day. He poured himself a drink while Kate, her back turned to him, busied herself unnecessarily with the fire.

"Was that quite fair?" she asked suddenly.

"Kissing your paid employee, you mean?" he said, employing a cool inflection which she knew only too well.

"Don't be deliberately obtuse," she answered impatiently. "I wasn't suggesting that you were amusing yourself with the housemaid, but I'm responsible for Victoria and she's not been around much."

"You're not, you know. Mr. Brown is responsible for her," Robert retorted provocatively.

"Oh, Mr. Brown! And how do you suppose he will react if he suspects my notable cousin has been making idle passes under my own roof?"

"Your notable cousin doesn't make idle passes, my love, so stop being angry and doing your best to wreck that nicely burning fire," he said, and she put down the poker at once and got up from her knees looking a little sheepish.

"Sorry, Rob," she said, moving over to the tray of drinks to pour herself a sherry, "I've no business to take you to task in what is virtually your own house, I suppose, but that little episode looked suspiciously like a pass to me, idle or otherwise."

He sipped his drink in silence for a moment, regarding her affectionately across the width of the hearth, then he said with a complete change of tone:

"Dear Kate, your concern for your ewe-lamb is very right and proper, but you should know me better after all this time than to suppose I would take unfair advantage. Today I progressed a little way because the sun was shining and your delightful young protegée forgot to keep stoking the ancient fires, but by tomorrow she'll have had time to reach your own conclusions, and hostility will take over. By the way, did you know your young protegée will be twenty next week?"

"Yes, of course I knew. Could you get down for the night, Rob? I've asked John Squires for dinner to try to make the occasion a little festive, but it won't be very exciting for Victoria."

"Sorry, it's impossible mid-week. I'll send her a birthday card instead."

"That won't exactly send her into transports! You might at least manage a handsome floral tribute. Do you know that child's never had so much as a bunch of violets as a gesture from Mr. Brown? A cheque comes from the solicitors on the appropriate occasions, but never anything personal, so you might trot round to your pet florist who kept Irene so well supplied and give them a nice expensive order."

"Really, Kate! You do want the best of both worlds, don't you?" Robert laughed. "If I followed up today's little pleasantry by sending flowers, it could put all sorts of ideas into her foolish head, as you should be the first to point out."

"I don't see why—" Kate began stubbornly, then caught his eye and joined reluctantly in his laughter. "Yes, I see what you mean," she said. "Oh, well, perhaps when you next come down we'll have a second party and crack a bottle of champagne. Only—"

"Only what?"

"Nothing that you mightn't consider an impertinence. Do you ever see Irene now that she's back in circulation again?"

"That was a very transparent line of thought. Yes, we meet occasionally at parties when I can get to them; yes, she is as lovely and sought after as ever; finally and in the hope of convincing you of complete recovery, I have no regrets except for the wasted years. Does that answer you?"

"Yes, dear Robert, and I won't worry again. I, too, have regretted the wasted years and grieved for you," she said just as Victoria ran down the little winding stairs in a corner of the room to tell them that supper was ready. Kate saw her hesitate on the bottom step before she spoke and mistook the quick glance she gave them both for one of belated embarrassment.

"Come and have a quick sherry before we go in," she said, holding out a welcoming hand. "Robert and I have been reminiscing shamelessly—a sure sign of encroaching age, so one's told. Robert, fill a glass for the girl and help yourself at the same time. Since it's Sunday supper and traditionally cold, we won't incur Elspeth's wrath by keeping it waiting, so come to the fire and warm up, Victoria —these late spring evenings can catch one out once the sun is down."

CHAPTER FOUR

VICTORIA had ample time in the watches of the night to review not only her own disturbed emotions but Kate's too, and as Robert had predicted, by the morning hostility had returned. He was stopping over Monday as a brief concession to overstrain, and her elaborate manoeuvres to keep out of his way apparently passed unnoticed. He made no attempt to seek her out.

John Squires looked in on them before lunch to run a professional eye over Timmy, evidently surprised and not too pleased to find the weekend guest was still with them. Victoria liked the quiet, uncommunicative doctor who was a widower with a growing practice in the district and, listening to the two men's casual exchanges over their beer, realised that neither much cared for the other. She had long suspected that John Squires had more than a friendly interest in Kate and no doubt resented Robert's easy claim to her hospitality, but familiar now with the betraying nuance which could creep into a desultory remark almost unnoticed, she thought that Robert, too, was not immune from the natural antagonism of the possessive male.

"Still waiting and hoping, seeking no reward but the comfort of your smile and, presumably, the periodical settling of his bill?" Robert said when the doctor had driven away.

"Don't be so absurd, Rob! John takes a great interest in Timmy and has always thought that something could be done about that leg when he's older," Kate said a little brusquely, but she flushed very slightly and Victoria, because she considered that if he was aware of Kate's feelings for himself, Robert had no right to make fun of her in this fashion, remarked with some tartness:

"It's easy to jeer at qualities one doesn't possess oneself."

She should have kept her mouth shut, of course, for Robert turned round to look at her absently as if he had

forgotten her presence and observed with amusement:

"Dear me! Is it possible that you, too, have fallen a victim to the good doctor's hidden virtues? Kate, you must look to your laurels in the face of unexpected competition."

"Be quiet, Robert! Your humour is ill-placed since it's obvious neither of us has anything but honest liking for a very good friend. I don't know what's got into you since yesterday," Kate said with most unusual asperity.

"I must have got out on the wrong side of my bed, as they say in the nursery," he replied meekly. "And here's another who made the same error, didn't you, Victoria Mary?"

"I'll go and get Timmy cleaned up for lunch, Kate," Victoria said, pointedly ignoring him, and went out of the room.

"You see!" Kate said as the door closed with the faint suggestion of a slam.

"What am I supposed to see? A little girl who takes teasing as a personal affront when she should know better?"

"I'm not at all sure that wasn't your intention. You may be regretting your lapse of yesterday, Robert, but you don't need to rub it in by being deliberately hurtful. Victoria may be inexperienced, but she has enough savoir faire to take such things at their proper value."

"What things?"

"Oh, don't be so tiresome! I was only trying to say that she's unlikely to have taken your advances seriously."

"Advances—what a delightfully old-fashioned expression! But only yesterday, sweet Kate, you were trying to convince me of the opposite. Putting ideas into her head, you said."

"On the contrary, it was you who said that when I suggested you might send her some flowers for her birthday."

"So I did. Anyway, don't you think we're making rather much of a very commonplace incident?"

"Not so commonplace in Victoria's reckoning, I don't mind betting. Now, will you do some chores in the village for me after lunch? Timmy is dying for a drive in your

50

new and opulent motor and you can take Victoria, too, and establish a truce."

But the outing was not a success. Before starting off Victoria, who had not wanted to go, viewed the Bentley's elegant lines without enthusiasm and when asked by Robert for her opinion, observed rashly: "Sleek and superior—rather like you," which she had to admit later was not a promising overture to friendly relations. Robert insisted on Victoria taking the wheel, thinking, no doubt, she would enjoy handling a quality car after Kate's ancient and sober old Morris. She had passed her test some time ago and was quite confident when driving the familiar Morris, but Robert's Bentley was a different matter altogether and he made her nervous.

"For goodness' sake, don't stamp on the accelerator like that! This car's a high-powered lethal weapon and will rocket us straight into kingdom come if you don't watch out," he exclaimed on one occasion.

"You do it on purpose for the fun of it—just the same way you enjoyed tearing strips off me that day in court," she said, and he was surprised to see tears in her eyes.

"Oh, come now! I don't enjoy the mishandling of a fine piece of machinery. It sets my teeth on edge," he protested, ignoring her accusation.

"Then why insist that I drive the beastly thing when you know very well I'm inexperienced?"

"I merely thought it would give you pleasure. Tell me, Victoria, is all this sudden antagonism a result of yesterday's charming little interlude?"

She sat very still beside him, blinking back the tears which already shamed her. She wanted to dismiss that episode as casually as he seemed to regard it and hurt him if she could for supposing that it might have meant anything more to her, but he unexpectedly cupped her averted chin in gentle fingers, turning her round to face him, and she remembered only the pleasure of his touch and Kate's overheard words as she came down the stairs.

"Dear Victoria Mary, don't turn me into an ogre just to satisfy your belief that there must be a villian in every self-respecting fairy-story," he said softly, and she smiled a little tremulously.

"I suppose Kate told you that."

"Oh yes, among other things. I suppose I should feel flattered that I unknowingly shared the honours with Mr. Brown in your flights of fancy, even if I *was* cast for the part of the Demon King."

He was smiling at her with that cajoling tenderness which only yesterday had surprised her into compliance, and she experienced a brief return of that curious desire to forget her preconceived notions and simply please him. She made a small gesture of hesitancy towards him, but they had both forgotten Timmy.

"Why've you stopped? What you want to quarrel for? Where's the Demon King? Want to *see* him!" he wailed, and when Victoria, remorseful at her own neglect, reached back to draw him to her, he struck at her outstretched hands, called her a rude name and started to bawl.

"That's enough, young man," Robert said, his laughter gone, and lifted the child over the back of the seat and deposited him in the road with one quick movement. "Now, Timmy—little boys who behave badly aren't wanted on motor drives. Are you going to say sorry to Toria for hitting her or do we leave you behind in the road?"

The boy stood, scarlet and hiccoughing on the grass staring up at his godfather, dimly aware that something besides his own behaviour had sparked off this unfamiliar anger, but unwilling to admit defeat.

"You—you wouldn't *really* l-leave me here, Uncle Rob," he spluttered, torn between doubt and defiance.

"Oh, yes, I would. It's time you learnt that boys don't hit girls, whatever the provocation."

"Toria wouldn't let you—besides, I'm lame. Lame boys have special attention."

"Toria will do as I tell her if she knows what's good for her, and you're no more entitled to special attention than other children. You were born lame, so you've known nothing different."

There was silence, punctuated only by Timmy's hiccoughing sobs and the cackling of hens from a nearby farmyard. Victoria, who had slid over into the passenger seat, made no further move to intervene but watched the small contest of wills with interest. It was rare in her experience for Robert to use his authority with Kate's son, but it was evidently not the first time.

The little comedy by the roadside came to an abrupt end when Robert reached out a hand to the dashboard and switched on the ignition. To Timmy, the sound of the gently idling engine was the final proof that desertion was imminent and without more ado he flung himself upon Victoria in a fierce abandonment of remorse.

"Good!" said Robert cheerfully, taking his seat behind the wheel. "Now that we're all friends again you shall sit between us in the front, Timmy, and if you're very quiet and good I'll let you steer between my hands."

Timmy, thus reinstated to a position of importance, held their attention all the way home, but once there he did not take kindly to being banished to the kitchen to take tea with Elspeth, and Kate, obliged to deal both with tears and Elspeth's ruffled feelings, was in no mood to bear tolerantly with her cousin's amused explanation of the original cause of the trouble.

"Yes, that's all very well," she said, for once finding no favour with Robert's handling of her son, "but Timmy isn't as strong as other children and when he gets over-excited, trouble can start. You at least should know that by now, Victoria—or were you too much engrossed with your own affairs to give a thought to your charge?"

The sudden attack was so uncharacteristic that Victoria was too taken aback to make any coherent reply and it was Robert who answered for her.

"Your young employee had been suffering discomfort on her own account, and might therefore be excused," he said on a faint note of irony, and Kate looked up quickly.

"And what might that mean?" she asked sharply, but he gave her one of his slow, tantalising grins.

"Not what you're obviously thinking, careful Kate. I had mistakenly urged the poor girl to try the Bentley thinking only to give pleasure, and she didn't take kindly to my comments on her driving."

There was a moment of rather flat silence during which Victoria could find no gratitude for Robert's intervention, then Kate gave a small apologetic laugh and hastily pressed fresh cups of tea upon them.

"I'm sorry, Victoria, I've been making mountains out of molehills, I'm afraid. Forgive me and have some more cake."

"Yes, you have, haven't you?" Robert said before Victoria could reply. "I wonder what can have provoked such an unusual display of feminine pique."

But Victoria had a strong suspicion, and since she judged by Robert's false air of innocence that he was equally aware of the answer, hostility rose in her again.

"Since you're a man you'd only recognise one reason for feminine pique, whatever that may mean, but women, let me tell you, allow small trivialities to upset a mood which have nothing whatever to do with the sexes," she said, putting down her empty cup and getting to her feet. "If you'll excuse me, Kate, I'll go up and read to Timmy until it's time to put him to bed."

"Well, there's gratitude for you!" Robert exclaimed as the door closed behind her. "I strive to excuse your employee's imagined shortcomings by stating the facts and get put in my place for my pains!"

"Serve you right, too! You know very well, Rob, that your intentions were anything but altruistic. You wanted to embarrass the child, didn't you?" Kate replied, and somewhat absently poured herself a third cup of tea.

"It's not easy to embarrass Miss Victoria Mary Hayes when her hackles are up, but I confess I find her unpredictable reactions rather endearing," he said, and received a straight old-fashioned look from his cousin.

"If I didn't know you better I'd have serious misgivings on the wisdom of encouraging these odd weekends," she said bluntly. "It would be a pity if you succeeded in turning the girl's head just because you find her unpredictable reactions rather endearing."

"Would you say there was any chance of her head being turned when the remembered image of the first Mr. Robert Farmer is forever looking over my shoulder?" he asked her with mock despair, and she shook her head at him.

"Don't play games just for the masculine satisfaction in breaking down resistance. It wouldn't be fair," she answered soberly, and the humour went from his face leaving it grave and suddenly tired.

"No, it wouldn't be fair," he said gently. "Don't anticipate contingencies that may never arise, sweet Kate; just remember that I'm grateful for the past years and your unfailing support and hospitality and wouldn't willingly give you cause for concern, imagined or otherwise."

"Dear Rob . . ." she said with a little smile of acceptance, "has the thaw set in at last?"

"The thaw?"

"That protective wall of ice you fashioned for yourself to shut Irene out. It's been so long."

"Yes, I suppose it has. Well, don't be too hasty with your metaphors, my dear. If ice melts too quickly it leaves nothing behind but a puddle of dirty water—no solid foundation on which to build again—so leave me a few stubborn icicles to bolster up my morale," he said with a return to his old manner, and she knew that the moment for confidences had passed.

"Well," she said, "I'd better go up to the nursery and do my share of story-telling. Will you come up later to say good night? Timmy's very jealous of his Uncle Rob's attentions."

"Yes, I'll be up. I don't think you'll find my halo's slipped, you know. Timmy was quite aware that he was being not only rude but wrong in hitting out at Victoria."

"Yes, and of course you were quite right to check him. I don't know why I made such a thing of it."

"Don't you? Well, never mind. It's been rather an unsettling week-end altogether, so perhaps we've all been acting a little out of character."

But although with Robert's departure the next morning the household appeared to settle back into its normal quiet routine, Victoria was conscious of change. Perhaps she imagined a slight withdrawal in Kate and only fancied

55

a certain coolness in Elspeth, but she found herself hoping that pressure of work would keep Robert away from Farthings for a time, for not least of her doubts was the curious effect on her own emotions. She did not flatter herself that his behaviour on Sunday afternoon meant any more than an impulse of the moment born of idleness and a masculine desire to experiment, but she wished now that she had slapped his face in the traditional manner instead of responding with such undisguised pleasure.

With the dawn of her birthday, however, such fancies were dispelled by the goodwill and small attentions surrounding her. Kate, very conscious that their quiet country life offered little in the way of excitement to a young and attractive girl, had tried to make the day a festive one with small surprises and presents hidden in unlikely places, just as she planned for Timmy on like occasions, and Elspeth contributed with a splendid cake ablaze with twenty candles.

The morning's post had brought the usual small cheque from the solicitors, together with the customary handkerchiefs from Scottie and Robert's promised birthday card. Kate privately thought Robert might have found time to choose a personal gift, knowing that Victoria had no relations to remember her, but if Victoria was disappointed there had been no time to dwell on it, for all her pleasure had culminated in the biggest surprise of the morning. Five dozen red roses had arrived by special delivery packed with all the extravagant trimmings of ribbons and bows and a card attached by a silver cord which read simply: *With the compliments of Mr. Brown.*

Amazement turning to pure bliss had illuminated the girl's thin face with such startling happiness that Kate had known a prick of irritation. It was absurd in this day and age that flowers from a perfect stranger should evoke such astonished delight.

"Well, it's a handsome gesture, even though some might call five dozen of the best a trifle excessive," she had said with some dryness, but Victoria had only smiled and alternately stroked a petal and the plain white card with equal tenderness.

"It wouldn't have hurt him to add a message—many happy returns or even just best wishes," Kate went on, wondering why she should feel so put out, and Victoria smiled again, the affectionate smile an adult might bestow on a complaining child.

"He never adds anything but his name," she said serenely, "I suppose the lawyers see to it for him, but he's never sent me flowers before, so perhaps, this time, he chose them himself."

"Hardly, when it's simply a matter of picking up the telephone, stating your requirements and leaving the rest to the florist. Is it his writing on the card?"

"I don't know. He never writes letters. The only other time he sent me a present Mr. Chapple or Mr. Ponsonby signed the card."

"Then the florist's assistant probably did the same. It's not a particularly distinctive hand. Never mind," she added hastily with a belated resolution not to spoil the day, "nothing can take away the compliment of five dozen expensive hothouse red roses to grace our rooms, so I, too, must be grateful to your Mr. Brown."

But she need not have troubled herself with regrets for her lack of enthusiasm. Victoria, her pleasure in the day enriched by such an unexpected tribute to her consequence, shared none of Kate's misgivings. The occasion was made perfect by the lavish abundance which greeted her eyes in every room, colouring her thoughts and filling the day with promise. Even Timmy, inevitably playing up at bedtime from over-excitement, failed to spoil the evening for her, though for Kate's sake she was glad when John Squires, arriving with a large box of chocolates to mark the occasion, went up to the nursery and restored peace with little apparent effort.

"You have as much influence over him as Robert," Kate told him with some surprise when later they were drinking their sherry while awaiting Elspeth's summons to dinner, and he gave her a rather curious look.

"Well, of course your cousin has the advantage of

57

occupying a pedestal, but even a dull country G.P. can cultivate a way with children," he replied with a twinkle, and Kate smiled demurely.

"You shouldn't grudge Robert his place in the sun—he's known Timmy ever since he was born," she said.

"Consequently the natural father-substitute in your eyes?"

"Not necessarily, but it's become rather a habit to depend on Rob. He's been a good friend to us both, as I think you know, and helped me through a bad time after the accident. I wasn't very good company then."

"Very likely, but you had no reason to blame yourself for the boy's infirmity."

"If I hadn't insisted on going in the car with Jim that day, Timmy wouldn't have been born as he was."

"That's only surmise. Shock can certainly cause damage to the unborn child, but no doctor would care to commit himself on the evidence in your case, so bury that bogey where it belongs, in the unalterable past."

Victoria had moved away, feeling she was eavesdropping as the conversation became unexpectedly personal, and she stood now in the shadows at the far end of the room, rearranging one of the many bowls of roses.

If the doctor had momentarily forgotten Victoria's presence, Kate had been perfectly aware of her tactful withdrawal and the mischief was back in her voice as she said: "You're quite oblivious of your social obligations when you get on your hobby horse, John. Here's our birthday girl politely trying to efface herself when you should be paying her compliments instead of forgetting it's her party."

"Victoria is much too sensible to take offence, since I'm neither particularly young or one of her attendant swains," he answered, quite unabashed. "But evidently somebody is sufficiently *épris* to spend a small fortune on flowers. I've never seen such an extravagant display of horticulture in all my life. Who is he, Victoria?"

"Only Mr. Brown, but as he's never done such a thing before, it's rather special," Victoria replied, coming back to join them again.

58

"What! The eccentric old gentleman who pays the bills but remains unseen? How very disappointing."

"Oh, no," Victoria said, her eyes bright with her inward thoughts, "it's crowned the whole day. Nothing that Mr. Brown has ever done for me has given me quite the same pleasure."

Kate said rather quickly: "I'm afraid Victoria, for all the advantages of being finished abroad, still tends to cling to her schoolgirl daydreams."

"There's nothing wrong with a bit of daydreaming—we all indulge at times—and even to my untutored eye, being finished abroad has paid off handsomely. It's a pity there's only myself here to appreciate the results," John replied with quiet sincerity. Indeed, he thought she looked charming and refreshingly free of the modern tendency to picturesque squalor, sitting there in her white, full-skirted dress, the soft hair with its demure centre parting falling in a shining curve about her neck and shoulders. She was the sort of daughter he would have liked himself, had he not been fated to be childless, and he found himself wondering what sort of a chap this unknown benefactor might be to content himself with periodic reports of progress and nothing more. By the same token his thoughts wandered to the possible effect a young and unspoilt girl might have on a man of Robert Farmer's calibre. He was aware that Kate's rather too well-endowed cousin was not without interest in her protegée, and he wondered, with mixed feelings, how long it would be before Kate herself became conscious that she might have dallied too long in making up her mind.

It was a relief to Victoria that Elspeth chose that moment to announce that dinner was ready, but her pleasure in Kate's well-intentioned plans to mark the day as something special was beginning to dwindle. It had been a mistake, she thought, to invite the doctor as the sole guest to lend the occasion a party air. She would have been better pleased to sit down with Kate as usual than make up an ill-assorted trio, and although John, doubtless aware that he had started the evening off on the wrong foot, made gallant efforts to amend his shortcomings, she was faintly

59

embarrassed by his avuncular attempts at chivalry. They drank champagne with rather forced gaiety and only Elspeth, summoned to join in a toast to Victoria, treated the occasion as a ceremony. But Elspeth, having excelled herself in the matter of choice dishes, was entitled to insist on ceremony despite the absence of guests, thought Victoria, and knew it would be useless to excuse herself tonight with offers of help with the washing up.

After dinner they watched television, that last standby for filling an empty evening, but John did not stay late, saying he had a call to make on the way home, and Kate made no effort to dissuade him.

"I'm afraid it's all been rather a flop," she said to Victoria as she emptied ashtrays and collected glasses after he had gone.

"Oh, no, Kate!" Victoria protested, distressed beyond measure that such good intentions should only bring disappointment. "It's been a lovely day and you thought up so many nice surprises."

"Rather as if you were Timmy's age and expected juvenile treats," Kate said, and there was a tinge of bitterness in her voice. "But your reactions were irreproachable, Victoria. Never for a moment did you let me feel I was treating you to nursery entertainments."

Victoria stooped to pick up a cushion and restore it unhurriedly to its proper place, then she said deliberately:

"What's the matter, Kate? It's not like you to have doubts without foundation. Is it John?"

"That was my worst mistake. I should have known better than to ask him because I felt you should have a party. It made a dull evening for you and a not very profitable one for him."

"It wasn't dull, just a little out of my element. I think John's in love with you."

"I know. He's a dear and good and dependable and I owe him so much for his care of Timmy, but sometimes—"

"Sometimes those very virtues work against him."

"Yes, they do, but how can you know?"

"I don't really, but I can imagine. Scottie was rather like that, you know, and Father never really appreciated her. I like your John. I don't find him dull."

"Neither do I, oddly enough. I'm past the age of demanding pretty speeches and scintillating wit in an admirer, and John would make an excellent husband. His own marriage was a failure, so he wouldn't expect too much."

Victoria considered this aspect carefully before answering. She could not altogether feel that not to expect too much was a virtue, but on the other hand, her own upbringing had taught her the virtue of security and having someone in the background to depend upon, even though it was only the intangible presence of Mr. Brown.

"Well," she said then, "I wouldn't know about marriage, of course, but I would think there should be something more than just mutual tolerance."

"Mutual tolerance is very important, let me tell you, but then you're young and romantic fervour would naturally come first. Don't look as though I'd insulted you, darling—it's only right at your age to think no further than falling in love and living happily ever after."

"I don't think I do—think much about falling in love, I mean. If I marry I would certainly hope to feel rather more than mutual tolerance for my husband, but I've already learnt that other people seldom have the same needs as oneself."

"Well, don't go ascribing false needs to the self-sufficient Mr. Brown on account of one uncharacteristic gesture. I doubt if the flowers mean any more than a belated act of conventional politeness," Kate said, speaking more brusquely than she meant because Victoria's uncertain future had begun to trouble her.

"Of course not. All the same—" The telephone rang, cutting short Victoria's response, and Kate went to answer it, rather relieved that these slightly disturbing exchanges should be broken, but impatient with John Squires, whose voice she expected to hear, for thinking it necessary to apologise for the party's failure. But it was not John, and

61

she handed the receiver over to Victoria, saying a little irritably:

"It's Robert for you. A little late with his birthday greetings, but at least he remembered to send a card." She did not leave the room but resumed the small chores she had started at the beginning of their conversation. If she listened for any betraying nuances in Victoria's replies, it was quite unconscious, but Victoria, remembering the look on Kate's face that Sunday afternoon, felt awkward as she answered Robert's father frivolous enquiries as to how the party had gone.

"It was a pity you couldn't be here," she said a little coolly. "It would have been so much nicer for Kate to have even numbers."

"By which do I gather that the worthy doctor paid all the attention to you and none to poor Kate?"

"Certainly not. In point of fact—"

"In point of fact, it's you and not Kate who would have benefited by my presence for the feast. Did you play gooseberry?"

"Really, Robert! You have a very good conceit of yourself. As to your last remark, I had no chance to do anything else since it was my party."

"Kate's listening, is she? Well, what shall I say to provoke further tantalising observations from your end? Didn't the conscientious Squires rise to compliments or avail himself of any chaste avuncular salute?"

"No, he did not. Why are you being so nosey, not to say infuriating?" Kate gave a faint, unmatronly giggle and Victoria made a face at her.

"Naturally I'm nosey about what goes on in my absence. I have prior claim in the matter of chaste salutes. Are you being unfaithful to me?"

"Have you been drinking?" she snapped back so sharply that Kate looked round in surprise.

"No, no, I'm most regrettably sober, not having had your excuse for champagne," he answered. "I was only trying to imagine the festive scene. If there was no excitement beyond Elspeth's doubtless lordly offerings, what *did* you do with the rest of the evening?"

"We watched television," said Victoria primly, and felt herself colouring at his burst of ribald laughter.

"Well, well . . . I should certainly have been with you to put a stopper on that. And did you have some nice presents?"

"Very nice, and thank you for your card. Did you choose it yourself?"

"Certainly. I thought hearts and flowers very appropriate."

"Did you? I can't think why." But the mention of flowers distracted Victoria from thinking up retorts to put him in his place and she added in quite a different tone of voice: "And what do you think, Robert? I had five dozen gorgeous red roses from Mr. Brown by special delivery."

"Did you indeed? So the Sphinx has spoken at last, has he? And that, of course, made your day, and probably encouraged unlikely fancies," he answered, and the mockery in his voice came to her very clearly over the line.

"It made my day, certainly, but I'm a little old now to cherish unlikely fancies," she said, and Kate, with a quick glance at her face, at last left the room.

"Of course you are—twenty and done with the foolish pretence of childhood, but no doubt you have changed them for other and more romantic expectations suitable to your new estate."

"You," she shouted down the telephone trying to disguise a sudden desire to cry, "are as unfeeling and—and beastly as you were that day in court, mocking and—and brow-beating just for kicks. Why don't you pick on someone your own size?"

"Has Kate gone?" he asked with seeming irrelevance. "Yes? I thought she must have or you wouldn't have dared to talk to me like that." But he must have heard the tremor in her voice, for his own suddenly lost its provocative raillery and became gentle. "Don't think badly of me, dear Victoria Mary. The habit of levity grows upon one as a necessary defence. I have no wish ever to hurt you by banter, so bear with me kindly if you will."

His capitulation was so unexpected and the warmth in his voice so beguiling that her tears waited no longer.

"Are you crying?" Robert asked after a long silence, and when she answered "No" in a suspiciously shaky voice, he swore softly at the other end of the line.

"Now I've spoilt the day for you. Go on hating me if it eases you my child. One day I'll hope to show you a different Robert Farmer. Till then, dream your dreams and fight your dragons to your heart's content. Good night, now, and a belated but very sincere many happy returns."

He had rung off before she had time to thank him or adjust her mood to his and as she turned to replace the receiver she saw Kate standing in the doorway watching her.

"Well, have you made your peace?" she asked, but her voice held none of its usual indulgence and Victoria was again reminded that where Robert was concerned Kate had very definite reservations.

"I suppose I should know him better by now than to take his teasing seriously," she answered evasively.

"Yes, you should. And that could apply to other things, too. It would be a pity if you allowed your head to be turned for want of a little wordly experience."

Victoria stared at her, the tears still bright on her lashes, and felt the colour begin to creep up under her skin.

"Kate," she said gravely, "I'm not so inexperienced that I'm likely to read more into a casual incident than was intended."

For a moment Kate looked embarrassed as if she had not expected to be met with such a direct response, then she rubbed her eyelids as though they ached and sat down on the arm of a chair.

"I'm sorry, Victoria, I shouldn't have said that," she replied, sounding suddenly tired. "I'm very fond of Robert, you see, and I wouldn't like him to be hurt all over again."

All at once Victoria lost her temper.

"Why can't you come straight out with it and tell me not to trespass?" she demanded. "If it gives you any comfort, Robert is the last man who would turn my head, so don't let a casual kiss disturb any personal claims. If he flatters himself he's made an easy conquest then you can disabuse him in no uncertain terms. I'm sorry you happened to witness that incident, but don't lose any sleep on his account or mine."

"Oh, dear! I have made a mess of things!" Kate said, looking defeated and rather surprised. "I'm afraid you've completely misunderstood my well-intentioned efforts, but, unlike everything else today, I seem to have made errors of judgment."

She sounded so tired and unsure of herself that Victoria immediately felt ashamed of her outburst

"I'm sorry," she said, "I shouldn't have spoken to you like that, Kate. You've made me feel so much one of the family that it's difficult sometimes to remember my place."

That made Kate laugh and she stretched out a conciliatory hand.

"What an idea! Your place is here at Farthings and has nothing to do with employment. And if you can bring yourself to accept Robert along with Timmy and me, I for one will be grateful to you." It was graciously spoken, Victoria thought, considering the probable state of Kate's affections, and she would have liked to assure her that far from leading Robert Farmer up the garden she had every intention of discouraging further opportunities when next he came to Farthings. But too much had already been made of a situation that should never have arisen and she could only smile apologetically and take herself off to bed.

CHAPTER FIVE

IT was June before Robert paid them another visit and despite her hope on the last occasion that pressure of work would keep him away, Victoria found that she had missed him. Kate's circle of acquaintances was small and consisted largely of young marrieds with growing families which kept them too busy for cultivating more than a casual neighbourliness, and sometimes Kate would look at Victoria a little ruefully and apologise for the dullness of country life.

"I've let myself drift since Jim died, I suppose," she said on one occasion. "Timmy occupied so much of my time when he was a baby that it was easy to drop out, and now I'm just selfishly content with my own company and the peace and pleasant monotony of Farthings. But you should be having fun, admirers like other girls and justifying the expense of that finishing abroad."

"You needn't feel anxious on my account. It's still a novelty to have anchorage after years of being pushed from one select establishment to another and very restful," Victoria replied, sounding old-fashioned and a little pedantic, and Kate frowned.

"Well, I suppose that's natural considering the unusual circumstances, but I can't feel the aim of all this careful preparation was to bury you in the country where chances to benefit by it are few," she said, and Victoria laughed.

"Well, I wasn't being prepared for a London season and the chance of an eligible husband, if that's what you're thinking was the aim—unless of course it was Mr. Brown's original intention and the idea just died on him."

"That's possible, I suppose, and rich cranks who indulge in the whims of the moment are notoriously unreliable."

"Do you think Robert knows who he is?"

"Rob? I shouldn't think so for a minute, and he'd know better than to abuse professional etiquette by pumping old Chapple to satisfy your curiosity."

"Yes, of course. Only sometimes he's so ribald about

poor Mr. Brown that I've wondered if he thinks he doesn't exist."

"Well, whatever he may think, five dozen roses would seem to settle that doubt. Have you had any reply to your letter of thanks?"

"Only from the solicitors, but they never do more than acknowledge mine. I *had* thought that as this was something more personal, they might have mentioned it, but I expect the roses, like the cheques, were just so much routine to them. When is Robert coming down again?"

She asked the question casually enough, but Kate glanced down at her curiously. She was lying on her back in the long grass by Kate's deck chair thoughtfully chewing a piece of clover and there was a withdrawn look about her as if she was indulging in one of her private fantasies.

"I don't know," Kate said, careful to sound equally casual. "Why? Have you missed him?"

"I suppose I have—like the way one misses a tooth when it stops aching."

"Well! Robert *would* be flattered!" Kate exclaimed, not knowing whether to be relieved or mildly indignant. "I must certainly remember to pass that compliment on."

Victoria giggled, unabashed, and rolled over on her stomach.

"Well, you know what I mean. An irritant keeps you on your toes even while you wish it would stop. I have the same effect on Robert, judging by his behaviour, so I'm sure he'd understand."

It was not the sort of remark to give Kate any real clue as to the measure of Victoria's feelings, but she had to admit to a superficial element of truth. It was, she thought, unfortunate that owing to Mr. Brown's liking for wrapping his protegée in cotton wool, the only man she was likely to get to know well should be her own cousin.

"Oh, well," she said a little helplessly, "if you feel Robert is neglecting us, you'd better write yourself and suggest a visit. I had a notion that his reasons for stopping away were not entirely unconnected with yourself."

"I could hardly do that since it's your house and he's your guest," Victoria answered with a polite air of rebuke and impatiently tucked her hair behind her ears to stop it from tickling her.

Kate observed those faun-like features with interest, remembering Robert's teasing, and said lightly: "A guest in his own house, not mine," and Victoria gave her a quick enquiring look.

"Well, it's yours for the present, since you pay rent," she replied, and would have liked to follow up the statement with queries about the future of Farthings when Kate's lease was up, but it might be premature to press for an answer, neither did she particularly relish a too definite reply.

"Yes, of course. Still there's always been an understanding that he should treat the place as his home, so he'll come without being asked when the mood takes him," Kate said with an air of closing the subject, and Victoria thought she sounded a little short.

During the week, however, it was easier to avoid the unwelcome thoughts which these chance remarks could cause to flourish unsatisfied. Kate, on the final chapter of her latest book, was closeted with her typewriter for long hours, and Victoria, in sole charge of Timmy, delighted in sharing in his games and inventing fresh amusements of her own.

John Squires, who privately considered Kate's concern for her son excessive, if understandable, approved the ease and youthful casualness with which Victoria handled the boy.

"You'll make a charming mother when your time comes," he told her once when he had met them in the village and paused for a chat. "You'll not grow old in heart like so many women. Do you want children of your own?"

"Oh, yes, but first I have to find a husband," Victoria replied demurely, but her eyes were dancing. She had always found it very easy to get on with the doctor when she had him to herself.

"Well, that shouldn't present any difficulty. If I was a younger man—" he said, shamelessly dismissing Kate's image in an effort at gallantry which Victoria found rather touching.

"You say the nicest things, John, but I know where your true heart lies," she said affectionately.

"Do you indeed? Well, it's your prospects we're discussing, not mine, and I have to admit there's not much choice to be had in these parts. How long will you be staying with Kate?"

"As long as she'll keep me—if that is, the solicitors allow it. It's supposed to be a trial run, you know."

"Ah, yes. The omniscient Mr. Brown who pays the piper and calls the tune."

She looked at him and her eyes were startled.

"Yes, I suppose that's the whole answer," she said, sounding surprised. "Well, in less than a year the piper will have been paid off and that will leave *me* to call the tune."

"So . . . and what are your plans?"

"I haven't any. It wasn't any use making plans for earning a living. My suggestions were either stamped on or there was a last-minute postponement. It was really a most unexpected concession to be sent here, but I suppose Kate's credentials were so exemplary that no objections could be raised."

"Or your Mr. Brown is shrewder than you think. Not much chance of unwelcome competition in a village as remote as this."

"Competition? But there's nothing personal in the arrangement. I've never even met him."

"For all that, I understand a pretty observant eye has been kept on your activities. If admirers are to be discouraged, Farthings is a pretty safe place for a young girl's first job."

"Yes, I suppose it is, only there doesn't seem much point, does there, if when the Trust is wound up I'm free to do what I like?"

"No, it doesn't sound very logical, but who's to know what twists and quirks govern the actions of rich eccentrics with a taste for power?"

Victoria giggled: "You make him sound rather sinister —a kind of Svengali chuckling in the wings and casting spells."

"Farmer hasn't been down for some time. When is he next expected?" John observed casually.

"I don't know. I believe the lists are very heavy for this term," Victoria said, and he glanced at her speculatively.

"H'mm . . . Kate seemed to have an idea—still, she could well be wrong."

"Kate, like anyone else, can jump to wrong conclusions," Victoria said, choosing her words carefully. "She's been working rather long hours lately, finishing the latest children's epic, and imagination can carry over into real life without much distinction."

"You're a wise child, aren't you, Victoria? I wonder how you came by your perceptions so young," he said, looking down at her with a measure of wryness.

"Well, when one's self-appointed mentor is never there to give counsel, I suppose one learns to seek it in oneself. Poor Mr. Brown! What a lot he's missed by sitting on a horse so high that they're both lost in the clouds," she said, deliberately making light of the matter, and he smiled, his blue, observant eyes momentarily losing their thoughtful gravity.

"Yes, poor Mr. Brown!" he echoed with his mock solicitude. "What a strange, unloved individual he must be, if that is, he exists at all, outside that fertile imagination of yours."

"Well, *someone* exists. I haven't imagined the monthly cheques and the other evidences of a directing power," Victoria retorted, and as if she had invoked some mysterious agency to give credence to her statement, a second delivery of roses arrived the very next day with an identical card attached.

This time the roses were pink, but their number no less extravagant, and Kate, observing the girl's heightened colour and the tenderness with which she arranged her flowers, felt a shade uneasy. It was not fair of Mr. Brown, whoever he might be, to start playing games of this kind, she thought, and wondered for an unreasoning instant if the thing could be some kind of crazy hoax on the part of staid old Mr. Chapple.

"Well," she said trying to sound flippant, "if this sort of thing goes on, you'll be raising false hopes again of a happy-ever-after ending," but Victoria smiled at her with that secret air of withdrawal and replied gently:

"Oh, no, Kate, I don't live in a fairy tale any longer, but you'll have to admit that, however disinterested this sort of gesture may be, it at least has the virtue of adding to one's stature."

"What a queer mixture you are," Kate said, reassured but not wholly satisfied. "Sometimes you talk like a woman twice your age, but I get your point regarding the tonic action of floral tributes, whoever they may come from. You're growing up, darling."

"Oh, no, I grew up a long time ago, I think," Victoria said reflectively, and Kate sighed, aware that there might be a rather sad truth in this observation.

"Yes, perhaps you did," she agreed, remembering her own childhood secure in the ties of a family united in love and wellbeing. There had not been the money to afford her the educational advantages bestowed upon Victoria, but neither had she been obliged to create images for herself in return for the chilly dispensations of an unknown benefactor.

Kate was to spend the following week-end in London which made quite a break in the household's routine, but her book was finished, her publishers anxious to discuss a fresh contract, and John Squires had been urging a short change of scene for some time. There was no reason to worry about Timmy with Victoria in charge and himself within easy call, he had said.

Victoria drove Kate to the station, attending gravely to the last-minute instructions of an anxious mother, solemnly offering assurances in the matter of her own competence until they both began to giggle.

"I'm not naturally a fusspot," Kate excused herself a trifle sheepishly, "but it's such an event for me to leave

71

Timmy just to go on the razzle that I suppose I'm reverting to type. Are you sure you won't be lonely, Victoria? I wish there were a few nice young people you could ask over to Farthings to keep you company."

"For heaven's sake stop feeling guilty because you're treating yourself to a holiday!" Victoria told her. "If you want to know the truth, I'm looking forward to playing mistress of the house in your absence and pretending Farthings belongs to me. I would be most intolerant of nice young people distracting me from my simple pleasures, so you can be thankful we don't know any."

So Kate went away satisfied and refrained from a warning not to build dreams round Farthings, a much more tangible fantasy than Mr. Brown, and Victoria drove home with a mounting sense of delight in the novel experience of being answerable to no one but herself for the next two days.

Elspeth had prepared a cold lunch for them set out in the shade of the patio, and afterwards, with Timmy settled on a lilo for his rest instead of being sent upstairs, Victoria wandered through the rooms of the house, enjoying her game of pretence. Here in the drawing-room filled with the elegant cabinets of china and bibelots treasured by that unknown maiden lady she would entertain friends after dinner; here in the cool flagged hall, masculine belongings would clutter up the brassbound chest, together with the discarded toys of children, and here in the white-panelled parlour she would sit and dream when she grew old and remember the follies of her youth with gentle amusement . . .

"There's no call to run your finger along the mantelshelf for dust, for it was done the morn," Elspeth's voice observed disapprovingly behind her, and she jumped.

"I wasn't thinking of dust," she said, her mind still focussed on that other world. "I like to touch things for remembrance."

"Are you thinking of leaving us, then? That'll no be good news for Mrs. Allen to come back to. I'd thought you were different to those foreign hussies who'd up and go as soon as they'd unpacked their traps for want of a

72

gay time." Elspeth spoke in the uncompromising tones that Victoria first remembered and she said quickly:

"Oh, *no!* I was—was only storing up memories for much later on. Sometimes, you see, I pretend to myself just to make things seem real—like inventing personalities for Mr. Brown."

Elspeth gave her a curious look and her eyes narrowed in dry comprehension.

"Making believe you're mistress here and planning your alterations, I suppose," she said, dismissing Mr. Brown whose existence she privately doubted, and Victoria, if a little astonished at being so promptly understood, hastened to disabuse her.

"If that were true and not just a game, I wouldn't alter one single thing. My plans were just make-believe too—imaginary domestic pictures, like children's toys scattered about and pipes and old coats belonging to the master of the house."

"And who, pray, might he be, or hadn't you got so far as that?"

"Of course I hadn't. Only Farthings was real — the rest were ghosts—even me."

"You're forgetting mebbe that the place already has a master. There may come a time when Mr. Rab makes up his mind to settle here."

"With a wife?"

"Aye, with a wife, if it's not already too late for courting." Elspeth, having delivered her rather ambiguous parting shot, left the room before she could be questioned further and Victoria stood, her fingers still absently caressing the smooth, weathered surface of the mantelshelf, wondering if it had been intended as a warning.

The day was too fine, however, to waste time indoors indulging in unrewarding fancies and the rest of the afternoon passed pleasantly enough. Timmy was on his best behaviour, joining happily in whatever game Victoria thought up to amuse him, and was clearly enjoying the novelty of being left in her care while his mother was away.

73

John Squires looked in for a few moments before dinner to enquire whether Victoria was lonely and Kate rang up from London to satisfy herself that all was well at home. She had spent more than she should on clothes and had been squeezed into the latest triumph in expensive foundations which, though certainly doing something for one's bulges, would be too agonising to wear to justify the expense, she said. She sounded young and excited, was just off to a theatre following a chance meeting with a man she hadn't seen for years, and she hoped Victoria wasn't finding her solitary state too dull. She rang off without prolonging the conversation and Victoria put down the receiver feeling rather staid and elderly.

"You'll have your turn when the right man comes along," Elspeth said as she brought in the supper, evidently mistaking Victoria's absent manner of imparting this information for disappointment. "Is it Mr. Rab who's taking her to the play?"

"I don't think so. She spoke of someone she hadn't seen for years."

"Then let's hope it's no' that other one turning up like a bad penny," Elspeth sniffed, and went away before curiosity could be satisfied.

Victoria did full justice to the meal, musing happily on the events of Kate's day. She was pleased that Kate was not enjoying herself alone but secretly glad that Robert was not her escort.

When the supper things had been cleared she watched television for a while, but the programme did not accord with the peace and quiet of the summer night and she switched it off, together with the lamp, and curled up in a chair to float on a gentle tide of contentment and dreams which mingled so pleasurably with the scents and sounds drifting in from the garden.

She must have slept, for she had no conscious knowledge of hearing any sounds of a late arrival, but when she opened her eyes moonlight was flooding across her face through the uncurtained window and the tall figure of a man stood looking down at her.

"Well," said Robert Farmer softly, "the Sleeping Princess in the flesh, and floodlit, too. I was, alas, a little tardy with the traditional awakening, but I can soon remedy that."

He bent over her, his face etched in unfamiliar lines as the moonlight caught it. She was too bemused to do more than give him that slow, uncertain smile which sometimes seemed an echo of her secret dreams, and he kissed her very gently on the mouth.

"Well . . ." he said as he straightened his long back, ". . . that was a distinct improvement on your usual welcome. Perhaps I was wise to stop away."

She struggled into a more upright position, uncurling her long legs from under her to allow her feet a more decorous place on the floor, and stretched out a hand to switch on the lamp beside her.

"Why didn't you let us know?" she asked, blinking sleepily in the light.

"Because, as usual, I didn't know myself until the last minute. Has Kate gone to bed already?"

She stared up at him, suddenly aware of the awkward timing of his visit. Kate was so seldom away from home that it would not have occurred to him to make sure beforehand.

"She's not here. She's gone to London for the week-end and won't be back till Sunday evening," she said, adding with genuine regret for a wasted journey: "Oh, Robert, I *am* sorry!"

He ran a hand absently over his chin as if he suspected he needed a shave, but looked amused rather than disappointed.

"Well, that may be unexpected but no setback to my plans. I'll go and find Elspeth," he said, and left the room to return very shortly with an Elspeth already divested of overall and shoes and evidently preparing for bed.

"What's got into you, Mr. Rab?" she was saying a trifle crossly. "You've been later than this and not disturbed the household. You know very well your room's always ready and there's no need to announce your presence till the morn."

"Well, since Mrs. Allen is away, I thought I'd better have your approval. The local hostelry would hardly take me in at this hour, and I don't fancy a long drive back to London." Robert spoke with an air of humouring possible opposition, but Elspeth merely looked surprised.

"And what has Mrs. Allen's absence to do with that? You've no' considered the proprieties when she lived alone, and I'm still here to make your visiting respectable," she retorted. "If it's Miss Toria having doubts, she can make her mind easy. We're both of us paid employees here and not concerned with the habits of guests. I was just coming down to lock up, but perhaps you'll do it as usual before going up." She bade them both good night in matter-of-fact tones and retired upstairs once more, and Robert glanced quizzically at Victoria and asked with faint mockery: "*Were* you having doubts, Miss Toria?"

Victoria, who had harboured no such thoughts, being largely concerned with his disappointment at finding his hostess absent, replied with a certain asperity:

"Why should I? Kate will be sorry she missed you as you haven't been down for some time, but if you don't mind putting up with your own company, it's no skin off my nose. As Elspeth pointed out just now, I'm a paid employee and am not concerned with the habits of guests."

"How prim you sound, suddenly. Did Elspeth's pointed reminder sting?" he asked teasingly, and caught a glimpse of that inviting smile which she hurriedly tried to suppress.

"Of course not," she answered with amused indulgence. "She evidently thought I was having maidenly scruples and was putting me in my place. Would you like a nightcap, Robert, before you go up? You know where Kate keeps the whisky, so just help yourself."

"You know," he said, availing himself unhurriedly of the offer, "you've changed for the better since last we met. I was right when I said I was wise to stop away."

"I hardly imagine you were influenced by anything other than pressure of work," she replied, watching him run appreciative fingers over the delicately cut pattern of his Waterford tumbler and thinking what well-shaped hands he had.

"Don't you? But then you've never credited me with much sensibility. Have you missed me?"

She thought of her remark to Kate which had met with such amusement and smiled reminiscently.

"Oh, yes," she said. "You keep my wits up to scratch if nothing else. Kate is too calm and too kind to argue with to score a point and Timmy too young. You, on the other hand, are fair game since brow-beating witnesses is your stock in trade, and there's no need to consider your feelings."

He looked at her thoughtfully for a moment or two before replying, then he said quite gently:

"Haven't you lost that penchant for creating false images yet? A brow-beating counsel may have his feelings, even if it does serve as an excuse for working off old scores, but there comes a time when the game resolves into a one-sided contest. You are too intelligent, my dear, to cling so obstinately to old misconceptions."

She was aware not only of a disconcerting change in his attitude, but one of unexpected compliance in herself. From the moment she had awakened in the moonlight to find him bending over her, the old hostility had slipped away and she knew that although she might try to revive it by whipping up imagined grudges, the desire to sting him into retaliation would never be quite the same again.

"You sound," she said at last, "as if you minded what I might think of you."

"Certainly I mind. Verbal friction can be amusing and often stimulating, but I wouldn't be human if I desired nothing more than that."

"And do you?"

"Oh yes. I have, perhaps, a greater understanding of the real Victoria than you suppose. And, without wishing to sound complacent, you aren't I think, as indifferent to me as you would like to believe."

"I've never been that," she said quickly, uncomfortably conscious of his attraction. "You're hardly indifferent to a person you perpetually wrangle with."

"True, but has it never struck you that that in itself should be a warning? There's a very thin dividing line between hate and love, so we're told."

She met his quizzical gaze with a composure she was far from feeling. She was not so untutored as to confuse his meaning, but neither did she jump to romantic conclusions. She remembered Kate saying: *Robert is fastidious and you are very much to his taste, I should say . . .* This was seemingly not so unlikely as might have been supposed, but Victoria was no longer ruled by the fanciful flights of her adolescence, and Robert was probably no different from any other man in the matter of casual affairs.

"No, it's not what you're thinking," he said suddenly, and there was a decided twinkle in his eye as he observed her betraying colour. "All the same I *have* a proposition to make. Shall we, just for this one week-end, forget our differences and try getting to know one another instead? It's unlikely such a suitable opportunity for better acquaintance will occur again."

He put his half-finished drink on the mantelshelf and held out both hands to her, and she unhesitatingly gave him hers. His eyes were still quizzical but not cold at all as they searched her face and she found herself wondering why she had once built up such an unflattering image of a stranger she was unlikely to meet again.

"Am I to take it you're in agreement?" he asked, watching her changing expressions and trying to guess at her thoughts. "I'd like the chance to show you a different Robert Farmer from the one you've created for yourself."

"You said that when you rang up the night of my birthday," she said. "Till then, 'dream your dreams and fight your dragons', you said. What did you mean?"

"Just that the time wasn't ripe for the dragon's transformation. Like all the sorely tried victims of spells in the best fairy-tales, I was still condemned to enchantment."

"It sounds very odd for you to be talking like this— very odd and quite out of character," she said frowning.

"That, young woman, you have no right to judge until you know me better. Even brow-beating barristers have their moments of fantasy," he retorted and, releasing her hands rather abruptly, turned to pick up his glass again.

"What shall we do tomorrow?" he asked conversationally, firmly dismissing any further flights of fancy. At the same time he observed the lavish arrangements of roses which so far had escaped his notice, and whistled softly.

"Oho! More floral tributes! Has Mr. Brown been at it again?"

"Yes, he has," Victoria answered a little shortly, wishing for the first time that she could have presented Robert with the existence of a genuine suitor.

"Dear me, how remarkable! Are you celebrating another birthday?"

"Of course not. The lawyers probably slipped up and forgot they'd been ordered the first time."

"Very likely. Still, they've come at an opportune moment, for I, too, had notions of a belated celebration but no time, alas, to say it with flowers."

"Say what with flowers?"

"Happy birthday, of course. Kate suggested that when I next came down we'd have a second party and crack a bottle of bubbly. Well, I've brought the bubbly and a few recherché trifles, so we'll have to celebrate without her."

"Oh, Robert! That *was* nice of you," she said, flushing with pleasure like a child. "I will admit to you that everything fell rather flat that night. Poor John did his best, but he would much rather have had Kate to himself, and Kate was terribly conscious that it had been a mistake to whip up a spurious gaiety."

"Spurious gaiety . . . what a dismal picture that conjures up," he said with a wry grimace. "Well, I'll promise you this, Victoria Mary, there'll be nothing spurious about our gaiety, unless, of course, you've quarrelled with me by then."

"I don't think I shall quarrel with you, Robert," she said, rewarding his efforts with that sudden endearing smile and added curiously: "Why do you so often address me by both my names?"

"Because their prim respectability amuses me. Victoria Mary has a delightfully Edwardian flavour, and you with your demure centre parting and little nipped-in waist can look misleadingly decorous at times. No doubt I must thank your Mr. Brown for succeeding in shielding you from the pitfalls of this permissive age."

"Well, if I'm a milk-and-water miss you sound positively Victorian!" she exclaimed a shade indignantly. "Are you really old-fashioned, Robert, or do you just like to tease?"

"A little of both, perhaps, and I certainly wouldn't liken you to a milk-and-water miss. No well-brought-up young lady of earlier days would dream of being so free with her tongue and opinions," he retorted, and she giggled with what he told her reprovingly was an unbecoming lack of respect for his superior judgment and approaching grey hairs.

"Your judgment may be superior, my learned friend, but you're not old enough yet to demand respect as your right," she retorted, enjoying the small exchange with none of the old resentment, and suddenly liking him very much.

"Well, that at least should encourage my self-esteem. When one is over thirty one tends to get written off by young things in their teens," he said, and her eyes became thoughtful.

"But I'm not in my teens," she reminded him gravely, "I'm twenty and quite adult."

For a moment his eyes rested on her with an answering thoughtfulness and the lines in his clever face seemed to deepen and sharpen.

"So you are," he said then, "and in less than a year Mr. Brown's jurisdiction will be at an end. Are you going to miss this unseen influence which has coloured so much of your life?"

He had turned away from the light to rest his arm on the mantelshelf so that his face was now in shadow. She could no longer read his expression, but she thought there was a touch of irony in his voice.

"Yes, I suppose I will," she answered slowly, aware of a curious blankness lying ahead but not knowing how desolate she sounded until he moved impatiently and enquired whether she was still banking on that improbable happy ending.

"Not in the way I used to when I was young," she answered carefully, "but I see no reason why we shouldn't become friends, once we've met."

"And suppose you don't meet? Your Mr. Brown, judging by past eccentricities, is perfectly capable of vanishing into thin air if it suits him," Robert said, rather unkindly refusing to pander to hope.

"Then," she replied with fresh determination, "I should set about finding him myself, if only to say thank you and satisfy my curiosity."

"And how would you do that?" he asked with some amusement. "The lawyers won't betray a client, you know, however charmingly you may try to wheedle."

"I wouldn't waste time trying to wheedle Mr. Chapple, stuffy old bore," she replied with her nose in the air. "There are better ways of finding out — private eyes for one. It can't be so difficult to trace a person of Mr. Brown's peculiar habits, for he's sure to have other benevolent schemes on hand. Also, there's bound to be someone willing to give him away for a small consideration."

Robert burst out laughing.

"Well, for pity's sake! Private eyes and mercenary inducements! And how do you suppose such methods would endear you to your erstwhile patron?"

"Yes, that's a point," she admitted, looking crestfallen, but she rallied at once as her eyes came to rest on the roses' mute assurance of an awakening interest.

"You won't blight my expectations with legal objections, Robert," she told him cheerfully. "Those flowers and the others are my guarantee of good faith. There was no need, after all, to depart from the custom of years unless something more personal was intended, was there?"

He moved his hand with a quick, irritable gesture, knocking a china figurine on to the hearth where it smashed with a melancholy sound of finality, and Victoria went on her knees to pick up the pieces.

"Oh, dear, Kate *will* be upset!" she exclaimed, forgetting both Robert and Mr. Brown in this unfortunate mishap. "It was one of a pair she particularly liked."

"Nothing of the sort, she thought them hideous," he countered rather crossly, "but they belonged to my Aunt Eva and came with the house, so Kate tactfully left them where they were."

"Oh, what a good thing," Victoria said with relief, getting up and disposing of the remains in the waste paper basket. "I keep forgetting your aunt left everything to you. Nobody can complain if your break your own ornaments, can they? But returning to Mr. Brown—"

"I have no wish to return to Mr. Brown," Robert interrupted with unusual sharpness. "I'm heartily sick of Mr. Brown and I must beg you to keep him out of the conversation for the rest of the week-end, unless you want to try my patience too highly."

"*Well!*" said Victoria, her eyes growing wider and wider until her face seemed all angles and hollows, "of *all* things! If I didn't know you better, Robert, I'd think you were jealous of poor Mr. Brown."

"You don't know me at all as yet, so don't make rash pronouncements," he retorted, but the irritability had gone from his voice. "I think, however, we'll postpone our further acquaintance till tomorrow as it's getting late. Go to bed, Victoria Mary, and may your dreams bring sense, if not satisfaction. Good night."

CHAPTER SIX

IF she dreamed at all, Victoria remembered nothing upon awakening, but last night's promise of felicity remained with her, stirring a sense of expectancy for which she could not altogether account. The morning fulfilled the pledge of the day before with a heat haze already shimmering over the still countryside, and she resolved that nothing should spoil the day through retaliation on her part should Robert choose to provoke her.

There was no need, however, to guard her tongue. His teasing had lost its sting or, perhaps, she understood him better, and he very skilfully set about the business of proving her first conceptions wrong.

"You know, Robert," she told him as they lay soaking up the sun in the orchard after lunch, "I wouldn't have believed a month ago that I could feel so completely at home with you."

"A month ago you were intent on fighting dragons. I don't doubt the urge will arise again once the novelty of peaceful companionship has worn off," he retorted with his more customary dryness, but she only laughed.

"It isn't likely that companionship with you would remain peaceful indefinitely. You're too used to slapping people down in court to give in meekly," she said, and he reached out a hand to administer a more literal slap on one bare leg.

"And you, young woman, are too fond of trailing your coat to encourage meekness."

"Only with you. I'm really very accommodating in regard to most people. Ask Kate."

"Really? Accommodating is hardly a description that would appeal to Mr. Brown, I fancy."

"I thought his name wasn't to be mentioned over the week-end," she murmured demurely, and he raised himself on one elbow to look down at her stretched out beside him. Her eyes were closed against the sunlight which, filtering through the branches of an apple tree, cast provocative shadows across her throat and breast and the slender thigh exposed by the rucked-up hem of her cotton frock.

"Your innocent air of abandonment is curiously inviting — but perhaps you knew," he said softly, and her eyes flew open. She sat up abruptly, pulling her dress over her knees, and grace was suddenly lost in awkwardness.

"Ah, now you've spoilt it," he said regretfully, lying back again with his hands behind his head, aware at once that he had been premature.

"No, it's you who've spoilt it," she replied, remembering Kate's well-meaning hints. "I'm not accommodating in that sense of the word, I can assure you."

"Hush, child, don't pick a quarrel with me on that score," he said with lazy good-humour. "I spoke without consideration, for which I'm sorry, but you can set your mind at rest as to any dubious intentions. They're strictly honourable."

She caught the note of gentle mockery in his voice which he intended she should and immediately felt gauche and immature.

"I beg your pardon," she said with rather prim politeness. "I'm not at all used to remarks of that kind, you see. Mr. Brown has never encouraged followers."

He, in his turn, caught the veiled provocation in her last statement and propped himself once more on his elbow.

"Is that a direct invitation to quarrel? I thought we were agreed that mention of that gentleman might lead to trouble."

"Well, you mentioned him first," Victoria retorted, her resilience restored. "I was only trying to excuse a lack of savoir faire in myself."

"Were you, now? Well, despite the alleged scarcity of followers, you've no need to trouble yourself on that score, my dear. I suspect you'll have no difficulty in dealing with suitors when they start lining up."

"Suitors? Where?"

"Wherever you may happen to be after your next birthday — unless, of course, the unlikely occurs and you finish up as a substitute daughter after all — in which case," Robert concluded on a distinctly dry note, "your chances of selecting the man of your choice would seem to be rather remote, if past history is anything to go by."

She hugged her knees and giggled appreciatively, no longer ruffled by his tendency to poke fun at Mr. Brown.

"Well, since that contingency is equally remote, I won't need to please anyone but myself when and if the time arises," she said.

"*If?* Do you have doubts, Victoria Mary? I thought all attractive girls took a future husband for granted," he said lightly, and watched the untroubled look in her eyes change to one of grave consideration.

"I haven't really thought that far," she said, after some deliberation. "Time for me has been here and now, with everything arranged for me and my opinions not asked for. I suppose I've been too occupied in guessing at Mr. Brown's intentions to look ahead to any future without him."

"The gentleman is still an obsession, I see, despite this assurance that you've grown out of your infantile fancies," he observed none too sympathetically, and she smiled.

"Not an obsession, only a background and natural spur to curiosity," she replied. "However short of reality my infantile fancies may have been, he can't be dismissed as a figment of the imagination."

"You would be bitterly disappointed if he turned out to be no more than the collective contributors to a trust, wouldn't you?" he asked more gently, and she looked at him gravely as if she suspected him of possessing knowledge which she did not share, then smiled at him again rather abstractedly and replied:

"Yes, I would because it's comforted me to think there was someone who cared, even in an impersonal sort of way, what became of me. Even if your guess is right, you won't convince me those roses were thought up by a board of directors — or even a computer!"

"A computer . . . now that's a thought," he said appreciatively. "How would you feel if your elusive Mr. Brown turned out to be nothing more rewarding than an efficient machine?"

"You don't really think, do you—" she began, looking suddenly stricken, and he moved a little impatiently.

"Of course not, but I *do* think we've had enough for one day of that gentleman's tiresome intrusion into our affairs, to say nothing of the fact that, like all women, you aren't sticking to your bargain," he retorted.

"But we haven't quarrelled and I hope your patience hasn't been tried too highly," she countered demurely, adding as she saw him smile: "You really shouldn't generalise like that, you know, Robert. Women don't follow the same pattern just because they're female. You might find yourself in a lot of trouble one of these days by overlooking that fact."

"Might I, indeed?" he said with some asperity, reaching out a hand as if he meant to administer another salutary slap, but she twisted away from him, springing to her feet in one lithe movement of returning grace and stood leaning against the trunk of the apple tree laughing down at him.

He was reminded vividly of the occasion of their first meeting at Farthings when Kate had told her to take him round the garden and she had stood in the orchard shaking blossom on to her head with charming inconsequence while she spun him ridiculous yarns about Mr. Brown, imagining he did not remember her. He had, perhaps, been a little unkind in keeping up the fiction until he was ready to prick her innocent bubble of pretence, but he had been both surprised and piqued by the hostility she did not try to disguise, forgetting that youthful impressions went deep and tended to magnify with the years.

As if she, too, remembered and was deliberately recreating the scene, she stretched up a hand and picked off an overhanging apple, and a leaf or two settled on her hair.

"Not quite so effective as a shower of blossom, but nicely staged all the same," he observed, wondering if she knew how instinctively she had responded to his tentative overtures and whether she realised she was nearly ready to accept a new relationship, but she merely looked puzzled by his comment and bit into the apple with no sign of connecting the two occasions.

"Blossom?" she murmured vaguely, and had clearly not been listening. "Shall I pick one for you? They're not very ripe, but quite nice."

"No, thanks. Eve tried that one, too, but I prefer to do my own picking," he retorted. For a moment she looked enquiring, then she laughed, tossing the half-eaten apple into the long grass, and reached up for another.

"Oh, that old gag," she said. "I shouldn't be surprised if it wasn't Adam who did the picking, then blamed the whole thing on Eve."

"The woman tempted me . . . an unfair apportioning of the blame, you think?"

"Well, don't you? They say it takes two to make a quarrel, so I expect it takes two to share the blame. Anyway, it was really all the Serpent's fault and he got off without a scratch, which all goes to show."

"You talk a lot of charming nonsense, don't you? No, don't start on another. It would be a pity if our little celebration tonight had to be postponed because you had a pain in your somach," he said, getting to his feet and confiscating the fruit already half-way to her mouth. He picked a leaf out of her hair just as on that other occasion he had disentangled petals, but this time she did not try to free herself but stood looking enquiringly up at him, and he smiled and dropped a light kiss on the top of her head.

"We mustn't prolong this delightful idyll at my godson's expense or he'll feel neglected," he said. "Go and get him up from his rest and we'll play a game with him until tea-time."

Victoria hurried into the house, rather guiltily aware that with Robert's unexpected advent it had been all too easy to forget her responsibilities. She had devoted the morning to the boy while Robert drove to the village for extra stores to oblige Elspeth who, she informed him with slight asperity, had been counting on a quiet week-end with Mrs. Allen away and only Miss Toria and the bairn to cater for. She had looked with faint disfavour at the ready-prepared delicacies he had brought with him to augment their board and expressed the opinion that

Mrs. Allen was more likely to appreciate out-of-season luxuries than a young girl with little or no palate as yet.

"You forget the advantages of being finished abroad," he had reminded her with a grin. "If nothing else, young ladies about to take their places in society are taught discrimination in the matters of food and style."

"And what good will that do this poor lass with never a chance to show off her tricks at balls and parties and such-like?" Elspeth had demanded indignantly. "The daft old gentleman would have done better to have the girl trained for a sensible career than pay for fancy trimmings abroad to please himself."

"Perhaps he had reasons which will come to light in due course," Robert had answered, cocking a cynical eyebrow at her, and she gave an unmistakable snort, then smiled reluctantly.

"As to that I ha'e ma doots," she retorted, her accent broadening uncompromisingly as it did in moments of disagreement. "Still, you'll do no harm with your wee celebration if you mind your tongue and your teasing ways. It was no' a very gay birthday dinner with no man of her own to admire her looks and the doctor doing his best, poor man, to hide the fact that he wanted Mrs. Allen to himself."

"Would you say my cousin was—interested in that quarter at all?" Robert asked with rather deliberate casualness, and Elspeth gave him a distinctly old-fashioned look.

"That wouldn't be for me to remark on," she replied repressively. "I had my own ideas once, but mebbe I was wrong, and Mrs. Allen's no' the sort to wear her heart on her sleeve. Now don't waste my time any longer, blethering, Mr. Rab, when I've the lunch to re-plan to allow for one extra."

Timmy, with a child's sharp perceptions, had, when they all three met for lunch, sensed a difference in his two favourite grown-ups despite their joint efforts to amuse him, and now when Victoria came to waken him from his afternoon nap, he was ready to assert his rights by being contrary. His favourite games were no longer to his liking, neither it seemed was his Uncle Rab, making jokes he did not understand and taking too much of Victoria's attention.

Both Robert and Victoria did their best to keep him amused and ward off the probability of a scene at bedtime, but Elspeth's preparations in the kitchen together with Victoria's efforts to get him settled for the night in good time betokened something special in the way of a party from which he was to be excluded, and he took refuge in the only form of protest he understood.

Neither Victoria's blandishments nor his godfather's offer of a pickaback up the stairs could persuade him into compliance, for both of them were now out of favour, and he was making such a noise that none of them heard a car pull up outside or were aware of John Squires following his usual practice of entering the house unannounced until he spoke from the doorway.

At the time Victoria could only regard his intervention as mercifully opportune, for Timmy's tears stopped instantly and, with very little persuasion, he allowed himself to be hoisted triumphantly on to the doctor's broad shoulders and carried hiccoughing up to bed, but when he came down again to announce a little brusquely that the boy was quiet and ready to be tucked up for the night, she was not so sure.

"I used to flatter myself that I could always coax Timmy back to reason, but I seem to have lost my touch," Robert said, smiling a little wryly at the doctor, but John did not smile in return.

"Children are extraordinarily sensitive to atmosphere. The boy probably sensed he wasn't wanted," he said rather shortly. Robert raised a quizzical eyebrow but made no comment and Victoria protested indignantly:

"We've been leaning over backwards to keep him amused, but he got wind of the party and that finished it."

"What party?"

"Oh, not a real one — at least in a way it is. Robert had the idea of giving me a second party because he couldn't get down on my birthday."

"I see. A private celebration to make up for the awkwardness of the first. Well, I looked in for a while in case you should be lonely, but I can see I needn't have been anxious."

She could not understand why he should sound so stuffy, but it seemed clear that he had evidently been aware that Kate's party had been a mistake and she did not want him to feel hurt.

"It was a lovely party and not awkward at all. It was only Kate who minded because she didn't know any young men to make up the numbers," she told him anxiously, and was at last rewarded with an unwilling smile.

"That's nice of you, my dear—all the same, it's time you met young people of your own age and weren't obliged to fall back on Kate's old cronies for your entertainment."

Robert was busy mixing drinks and had his back to them, but he said over his shoulder:

"If that was a crack at me I take exception to being dubbed an old crony." He turned as he finished speaking, holding out a glass of sherry to the doctor, a faintly malicious twinkle in his eye. "You won't, I trust, be too disapproving to accept my wine and drink Victoria's health."

"Oh, dear . . ." Victoria thought unhappily. "Robert's in one of his infuriating moods . . ." That the two men were incompatible she had put down to their conflicting interests in Kate, but although John Squires' sentiments could well be guessed at, Robert's were less easily divined.

"Well now, since my cousin isn't here to set the conversational ball rolling, what shall we all talk about?" Robert asked, imitating the bright, encouraging accents of the professional hostess. "Victoria, you aren't drinking."

"I'll have mine later," she said rather hurriedly. "I must go up and settle Timmy and then it will be time to change my frock."

She thought Robert gave her rather a sardonic look as she turned towards the corner staircase in the parlour which was a short cut to the bedrooms and heard him say, just as she reached the top:

90

"You really shouldn't try to cramp my style by bracketing me with your own age group, my dear chap. I'm no beardless youth, I'll admit, but optimistic mammas still regard me as an eligible *parti*."

Really, she thought, suppressing an unseemly giggle, Robert could be quite impossible when he set out to provoke!

To her relief, she found Timmy sleepy and obligingly ready to forget his grievances. With an extra cuddle and the promise of something saved from the party to provide a treat for the morrow, he was content to let Victoria go without demur. She wondered how the two men were faring over their drinks, but she did not go down again and very soon heard John's car start up and, later, the sounds of water running into the bath accompanied by the familiar explosions emitted from the ancient boiler and Robert shouting down to Elspeth for fresh towels. He banged companionably on her door on the way back to his room to let her know the bathroom was free, and she went to perform her own ablutions, unconsciously renewing yesterday's game of pretence. With just such trivial domestic intimacies would she feel cherished were she mistress of Farthings, part and parcel of the masculine belongings and children's toys which she had mentally scattered about her make-believe home. It did not seem strange that Robert should now be playing an unrehearsed part in the fantasy, for although her imagined master of the house had been no more than a faceless figment in her mind's eye, Robert was not only very real but would one day claim the place as his own.

When she was dressed she stood in front of the long glass as she had on the night of her birthday and surveyed herself critically. She wore the same white dress, remembering how she had wished he could have seen her in it, and tried to view herself through his eyes. Would he find her pleasing, she wondered with recollections of his reputed fastidiousness, or was he too familiar with the image she had chosen to present to him to look upon her as a woman? It was, she supposed, unreasonable to desire his approval when she had shown so often that she was indifferent to it, but today had not been like any of the others.

The evening was all she could have wished it to be. Robert, who had put on a dinner jacket to grace the occasion, made every effort to charm her and succeeded so well that she found herself wondering why she had ever thought him cold and bitter-tongued.

"You were very rude to poor John who had only looked in out of the kindness of his heart, thinking I was alone," she admonished him as they went to dinner.

"Poor John was, I fancy, harbouring unworthy suspicions and deserved all he got," he retorted unrepentantly, and she giggled.

"Don't flatter yourself," she said. "He's only concerned with Kate's good opinion, not yours."

"Exactly. Now stop taking me to task. It's not becoming in you when I'm only trying to please," he said with mock severity, and seated her at the table with ceremonious courtesy.

He must have inspired Elspeth with a sense of occasion, Victoria reflected, for not only did she serve them an excellent meal but had set out the best china and glass and placed an old many-branched candelabrum in the centre of the table to add the elegance of candle-light to their feasting.

"What a shame Kate's missing all this," Victoria said, much impressed by all the festive touches, and Robert raised a sceptical eyebrow.

"Do you think so? Be honest, Victoria Mary, and admit that a small celebration *à deux* is infinitely more pleasing to you."

"How conceited you are!" she countered, but her smile held shy agreement and her eyes were bright with anticipation.

"But of course," he retorted, his keen regard capturing each changing expression and getting much enjoyment from her naïve responses. "Conceit is an essential part of one's armour if one wants to survive the rat-race—or if it comes to that, convince others of one's worth."

"I shouldn't have thought you cared enough to bother,"

she said, busily intent on extracting the very last morsel from her lobster thermidor.

"Ah, but then you're not acquainted yet with my secret aims and desires and the need to establish a footing — you really can't dig any more out of that empty shell, my dear child — didn't they teach you to restrain your unladylike greed in that Paris establishment?"

"Yes, they did, but I don't count you as polite society, so you must bear with my manners for just this once. Who do you want to establish a footing with? I should have thought you were well able to call the tune."

"Would you, indeed? And I'm not sure that I take it as a compliment to be excluded from polite society."

"Then you should, Robert. It only means that I'm at last feeling at home with you, and — and isn't that furthering this better acquaintance you've talked so much about?"

"In that case, I'm both touched and honoured," he replied gravely, "so don't take it amiss any more if I tease. Your first dislike for me was natural enough in the circumstances, but you're too old to carry a childish grudge into adult life, you know."

"Yes, I suppose I am, but it isn't easy to shed first impressions. Mr. Brown has dominated so much of my life in a remote kind of fashion, and you were all mixed up with the start of it."

"So you turned Mr. Brown into the traditional Fairy Godfather, and I was naturally cast for the Demon King. I should, I suppose, be flattered at having made an impression at all, though it was hardly the equivalent of a schoolgirl crush — or was it?"

He added the last provocative query so softly that she was taken off guard. She did not, however, immediately retaliate with outraged denials but sat staring absently beyond him while she deliberated with that thoughtful gravity which so often took him by surprise.

"I wonder if it could have been — in a topsy-turvy kind of fashion," she said then, slowly.

"Well, Victoria Mary, you never cease to astonish me!" he said, sounding for once a little at a loss. "I

93

would never have expected you to appreciate the psychology of that, much less admit it."

"Wouldn't you? That side of my education wasn't neglected, you know. The French take a deep interest in what makes them tick and we had to read up the accepted works in order to be able to converse intelligently at imaginary select dinner parties," she retorted, helping herself lavishly, from a dish of salted almonds, and his smile, if appreciative, was a trifle wry.

"Dear me! How alarming that sounds! And what else were you required to store away for the edification of imaginary guests?"

"Oh, the usual things — current affairs, the arts, of course, and the latest play or book. We were expected to be reasonably well informed on any topic of social interest, but never to air our views to the discomfort of the gentlemen."

Robert burst out laughing.

"Well, that should rule you out of court!" he said. "I've noticed precious little consideration for the gentlemen when you've had views to air."

For a moment she looked startled, then she sighed.

"You're quite right, of course, Robert," she said, reaching absently for another almond. "I suppose I never thought of you in that category."

"I see. You're informing me now that I'm no gentleman."

"Of course not! I meant the sort of young gentleman Madame imagined would be taking me out to dinner."

"Well, I'm taking you out to dinner now even though we're having it here at Farthings. Next time I'll arrange something smarter and more conventional, so you'd better get in trim for a proper display of all these social graces."

"Next time?"

"Certainly. This is just the curtain-raiser. On the next occasion you'll get the full treatment — the latest in fashionable restaurants, attentive waiters and a still more attentive host!"

"But—" she began, her eyes growing bigger and bigger,

but he reached for the bottle in its basket of ice to top up her champagne and said firmly:

"Now don't come out with the old statement that Mr. Brown doesn't encourage followers. It's time that gentleman ceased to be a convenient excuse, unless, of course, you have personal objections which you're too polite to state."

"Oh, no," she said very seriously, watching the bubbles dancing merrily to the surface as he filled her glass, "I would find it most exciting to be entertained by you, Robert. I'm sure you're very expert at the job once you've made up your mind the end in view is worth your while."

"Well, I'm not altogether certain that was intended to be complimentary, but let's drink to our better acquaintance just the same," he said with a wry little smile, then raised his glass to her and, for a moment, his eyes were grave and enquiring, belying the lightness of his words. She lifted her own glass in silent reply to his toast and her eyes held a shy promise of acceptance of which she was quite unaware.

Afterwards she could not remember very clearly how they had passed the rest of the evening, only that there had been sweetness between them and a growing sense of communion

They talked, covering a multitude of subjects; sometimes they just sat in companionable silence; once he stretched out a hand to tuck a strand of hair behind her ear, saying he found its faun-like resemblance vastly intriguing, and his fingers lingered, tracing the lines of her neck and bare shoulder with a delicate touch. The old house settled about them with its familiar nocturnal creaks and whispers and the first pale shaft of moonlight crept slowly across the floor. Elspeth could be heard moving from kitchen to dining-room laying the breakfast things for the morning, but she did not disturb them, and presently they heard her go upstairs to bed.

"And we, I suppose, should do likewise," Robert said, getting lazily to his feet. He stood looking down at Victoria curled up in the big chair, clearly reluctant to move, and held out both hands to her.

"Come along, my child. This is only a beginning and tomorrow is another day," he said, and pulled her up into his arms.

She stood expectantly between his hands, blinking up at him, her eyes already clouded with sleep, and reached up a hand to explore the sharply chiselled outlines of his prominent bones.

"I've often wanted to do that," she said.

"Have you, indeed? And why, might I ask, since you apparently found me so objectionable?"

"Only to make sure I wouldn't cut myself if I did," she retorted with a sleepy smile, and he caught her straying fingers, imprisoning them firmly against his chest.

"What impudence! For that you should be made to pay forfeit," he exclaimed, but when she obligingly offered him her lips, his mood changed. He cupped her upturned face gently between his hands and said softly:

"Have you understood, I wonder, that I've been making tentative love to you all evening?"

"Oh, yes," she answered serenely, "and most of the afternoon, too, I think."

"Oh, you do, do you? And have I made any progress?"

But her new-found consequence was weakening. Tonight she had been delicately courted with the sophisticated accompaniments of food and wine and the attentions of a man probably well used to easy conquests when he troubled to exert his charm, but she had no measure by which to gauge the depth of his intentions. He had teased her and kissed her, but made no demands on her charity other than that repeated desire for a better acquaintance, and she became painfully aware that the answer to his question must betray more than she was prepared to acknowledge, even to herself.

"Dear Robert . . . if by making progress you mean am I suitably impressed by your well-plannd celebration, then you've certainly earned full marks," she said, but refused to meet his eyes, and his smile held a trace of appreciative irony.

"Very nicely evaded, Miss Hayes, and I'm encouraged by such early signs of maturity. It's possible, though, that you have mistaken my intentions," he said, and was amused by the confused uncertainty with which she tried to withdraw from him. "Now, don't jump to extremes. As I told you this afternoon, my intentions are strictly above board, so there's no need for maidenly scruples."

"I'm not given to *them!*" she replied with scorn.

"You relieve me mightily! In that case, you'll doubtless take any future slip on my part in the spirit in which it is meant."

"What sort of slip?" The conversation was becoming confusing, or she was too sleepy and too content in her new-found felicity to follow him.

"Oh, just the occasional lapse into unrestraint which can overtake the impatient lover." He spoke lightly enough, but she was suddenly wide awake. Surely even Robert wouldn't carry his mockery to these lengths.

"Are you joking?" she asked, and the quizzical amusement immediately died out of his face.

"No, my bewildered sleepyhead, I'm not joking — just feeling my way. Do you find it so difficult to visualise me in the light of a lover?" he said, and the tenderness which she found so difficult to resist was back again in his voice.

"No — oh, no," she replied; then, because her conscience would continue to prick until she could silence those early unconfirmed suspicions, she added with naïve abruptness: "But what of Kate?"

"Kate?" He sounded faintly surprised, then one eyebrow rose a shade cynically. "Well, I shouldn't advise a spate of girlish confidences at this early stage. Kate takes her responsibilities seriously and tends to be over-anxious."

"That isn't what I meant."

"No? Well, whatever you meant, you can safely leave Kate to draw her own conclusions."

It was not, Victoria thought, a very enlightening reply, but short of asking him point blank if Kate had once been in love with him there was nothing more she could say to clarify the situation. She stood there a little hesitantly while he closed the windows and switched off the lights, and wished she had not rubbed off some of the evening's

97

magic by mentioning Kate. Perhaps Robert, too, was aware that something had been spoiled, for he opened the long window into the garden again and said:

"Come out for a few minutes before I lock up. It's a perfect night for making promises under the stars."

She went with him willingly, grateful for that touch of fantasy which seemed to bring him closer, and in the moonlit garden with shadows etched sharply across the dewy lawn and the warm air sweet with night-scented stock and new-mown grass, the magic returned.

They lingered for a while in silence, listening to the owls calling from the woods below and the myriad small night sounds which stirred in the leaves and grass about them, but he made no move to take advantage of the romantic setting and suddenly a brilliant point of light detached itself from the glistening galaxy above them and swept down to earth to be forever lost.

"Oh, look — a shooting star!" Victoria cried in delight. "You must wish, Robert. You must always wish on a shooting star, and this is the first I've ever seen."

"Then let's hope it's a good omen," he said, observing with tender amusement the way she instantly closed her eyes and moved her lips as if in unconscious prayer.

"Did you wish?" she asked anxiously, opening her eyes again, but he gave her no reply, only stooped to kiss her good night so lightly that she was scarcely aware of his lips touching hers.

"Bed," he said, brushing off a white moth which had settled on her hair, as long ago he had brushed away the white petals of apple blossom, then turned her gently back towards the house.

CHAPTER SEVEN

SUNDAY proved a sad disappointment after such seemingly settled weather, for rain had come with the dawn and the laden sky gave no promise of lifting.

"You'd never believe things could change so quickly after the heat of yesterday, would you?" Victoria said to Robert when they met for breakfast. "Everything seemed set fair for a lovely week-end."

"Which just goes to show that you can't trust nature any more than your own feelings," he replied with rather discouraging promptitude, and she eyed him uncertainly.

"What, exactly, do you mean by that?" she asked, wondering if he already regretted his mood of yesterday.

"Nothing very profound, merely a passing comment on life's depressing uncertainties," he anwered, extracting a wasp from the pot of marmalade and squashing it irritably on his plate.

"*Are* you depressed, Robert? The weather certainly isn't helping, I'll admit, but we can find plenty to do indoors and Timmy will welcome an excuse for his uncle Rob's undivided attention," she said, not realising how wifely she sounded until he cocked a sardonic eyebrow at her across the table, observing acidly:

"Trying your make-believe out on me?"

"Not consciously," she replied, making an effort to laugh at her own absurdities. "I suppose Kate being away gives me a false feeling of being mistress of the house, but it's only pretence."

"And what part am I playing in this pretence of yours?" he asked rather in the sauve, misleading tones he had employed for his cross-examination, but she was not going to be trapped into incoherent admissions or denials as she had been then, and replied coolly:

"I haven't got as far as casting you, yet. My imaginary master of the house is a very intangible character — just a dim figure in the background."

"Like Mr. Brown?"

"Not at all like Mr. Brown. I picture *him* living in some remote mansion in chilly isolation except for minions he pays so well that they never give him notice. I don't think he'd suit Farthings at all."

He laughed then and seemed to shed some of his early morning irritability.

"Poor Mr. Brown! I fear that his star is at last on the wane for want of a more substantial identity, and a good thing, too," he said, sounding rather pleased with himself, but she remembered the roses, undeniable evidence of an interest not wholly dutiful, even, perhaps, of a change of heart, and felt she had been unduly flippant.

"Oh, no," she said softly, "it wouldn't be a good thing at all. Even if we never met I should still feel bound to him in a queer sort of way."

The look Robert gave her was neither conciliatory or particularly sympathetic, but he spoke quite gently:

"In that case you seem likely to be caught in your dream world for the rest of your days. I wonder if you could meet this ubiquitous ghost the spell would be broken."

"What spell?"

"A spell you have made for yourself, I fancy, but no less potent for that. I'm not at all sure it isn't you who are awaiting for the traditional disenchantment and not me."

Despite the prosaicness of the breakfast hour and the discouraging sound of rain beating on the windows, something of last night's magic returned with his words.

"I'm glad you haven't forgotten all those things you said to me, even if you didn't mean them," she told him, and that unconscious smile began to turn up the corners of her mouth and then stopped abruptly as if uncertain of a welcome.

"I meant them, but possibly you misinterpreted my reasons," he said, but she answered quickly, instinctively avoiding a reply that could pin him down to more concrete explanations:

"There doesn't have to be a reason in make-believe— that's the beauty of it."

For a moment it seemed as though he would have liked to dispute the point, but he evidently had second thoughts, for he only shook his head at her and got up from the breakfast table to stand staring out of the window at the rain-soaked garden.

"Well, what shall we do with ourselves this uninviting morning? Shall we take advantage of the contrary weather and go to church?" he asked

"I should like to," she said, "but I don't think I ought to leave Timmy to his own devices, and Elspeth will be busy with the Sunday joint and won't want him under her feet. Why don't you go?"

"I think perhaps I will," he replied. "You didn't expect that, did you?"

"Well, you've never bothered much when you've been down before."

"To everything there is a season and a time for every purpose under heaven — or didn't your expensive education include a bowing acquaintance with the Bible?"

"Oh, yes, that was one of my favourites. A time to be born and a time to die . . . a time to weep and a time to laugh, a time to mourn and a time to dance . . . a time to love and a time to hate . . . practically everything's catered for, isn't it?" she said, delighted, if surprised by this fresh twist in his personality, but although his eyes softened as they momentarily dwelt on her eager face, his voice held a hint of asperity when he countered swiftly:

"A time to keep silence, and a time to speak . . . you've forgotten that one, possibly the wisest of them all. Well now, it's certainly time for me to get cracking if I don't want to be late for church, so I'll leave you to your nursery duties."

Up in the nursery, Timmy was contrary and inclined to be fretful, alternating between affectionate demonstrations which became a trifle exhausting and sudden withdrawals into silence which were equally difficult to treat with patience. Nothing she suggested for his amusement seemed to please him, and Robert returning from church with an hour before lunch to devote to his godson, fared no better. In the end his patience gave out.

"Very well," he said firmly but kindly, "since you prefer being rude and naughty to behaving nicely, you can have your lunch up here, instead of with us. Elspeth will bring up a tray."

"But it's *Sunday!*" Timmy protested, too astonished to resort to more usual methods for the moment.

"I know it's Sunday, but you should have thought of that before, shouldn't you? Come along, Victoria, we'll leave this naughty little boy to his own company. Perhaps we'll find him in a better mood after lunch," Robert said, extending a helping hand to Victoria, who was on her knees picking up tiddlywinks counters from the floor where they had been thrown in a temper.

"Well, perhaps if he says he's sorry, we'll let him come down after all," she said, aware that the boy, jealous and provoked, was quite quick enough to imagine he wasn't wanted.

"Certainly, if he's really sorry. Are you, Timmy?" Robert asked pleasantly. "Your mother won't be pleased, you know, if I have to tell her you've behaved badly while she's away."

Timmy, it was plain, had been wavering, but the mention of his mother brought his grievances to a head. He shouted. "*No!* I hate you! I want my mummy!" stamping his feet and bursting into angry tears.

"Oh dear!" Victoria exclaimed, wondering how best to quell the noise and offer comfort at the same time, but Robert said: "Leave him," in no uncertain tones and taking her by the shoulders pushed her firmly out of the room.

Down in the parlour, Robert poured out drinks and Victoria, accepting hers with the comment that she had earned it, relaxed in a big armchair feeling tired and rather discouraged.

"Have I slipped up somewhere, do you suppose?" she asked him a little anxiously. "I've never known Timmy to be so unreasonable before. I generally manage him so easily."

"Don't upset yourself. The boy's merely suffering from his first introduction to the green-eyed monster. It's time he learnt he's not the only pebble on the beach, anyway," Robert said. "Kate, with the best of intentions, keeps him too much apart from other children. You and she teach him his letters, I know, but there's no earthly reason why he shouldn't be attending some kindergarten school like others of his age."

"I understood John was against it. Kate sets great store by his judgment."

"The gallant doctor obliged with the desired medical opinion to establish his own standing, but he won't subscribe to sentiment much longer, from what I gather. Though we've little enough in common I have a great respect for Squire's professional integrity."

"Well, that's something of an admission," she retorted, eyeing him with faint disfavour. "Why, in that case, do you go out of your way to bait him?"

"For the same reason, probably, that you go out of your way to be upsides with me," he replied promptly. "Something in the worthy doctor brings out the worst in me."

She was silent, digesting the implication, then she said, sounding a little surprised:

"But I don't any longer, or haven't you noticed?"

"Oh, yes, I've noticed, my naïve little charmer, but then I've been exerting myself in no mean measure to that end, or hadn't *you* noticed?"

"That's rather a silly question, considering you must know the answer, but Robert—" she stopped, leaving the sentence unfinished with an unspoken question in the way she pronounced his name and his eyebrows lifted quizzically.

"But Robert what?" he asked, mocking her gently, and she looked away.

"Nothing, only—I wouldn't care to be just an experiment to bolster up your masculine ego," she said, and quite suddenly he became angry.

"How dare you credit me with such shallow motives out of your prejudice and colossal ignorance!" he exclaimed in his courtroom accents. "Do you imagine I'd waste my time trying to make a conquest of one stubborn little girl when there are those less averse to being charmed?"

She was a little shaken by such an unexpected reaction but not prepared to capitulate without a struggle.

"I may have been prejudiced, but I'm not so ignorant as to be unacquainted with the rules of human behaviour," she told him calmly. "I can imagine that if conquests, as you call them, have come easily, the one stubborn exception could present a challenge."

For a moment he looked as if her would like to shake her, then the hard lines about his mouth slackened and he laughed.

"Well, I'll give you this, Victoria Mary," he said, "for all your uncomplimentary opinions of my methods in court you need never number yourself among the browbeaten witnesses! I'd back you to stand up to the toughest cross-examination."

"But I didn't, did I?" she said, forgetting the present in being reminded of the ignominious past. "They told me afterwards my evidence had lost the case.'

"Who told you?"

"I forget. My father's solicitor, probably."

"Then forget that too. The case was lost before you ever went into the box and your evidence, even had you been better briefed, could have made no difference. It was just a last throw for leniency on the part of the defence, gambling on old Seldon's distaste for children being forced to give evidence, and it didn't come off. Had I been able to see you afterwards I could at least have relieved your mind on that score."

"I wish you had. I wish I'd known that you tried."

"Would it have made any difference to those uncharitable thoughts you've harboured ever since?"

"Yes, I think it would. There was nobody, you see, who seemed to care until Mr. Brown stepped in, and even he wasn't much use as a comfort, as I never met him."

"Yes, well . . . possibly he was afraid of involving you in some emotional entanglement out of a sense of obligation that you might later regret," Robert said absently, and she looked at him in surprise.

"Do you know, Robert, that's the first time I've ever heard you refer to Mr. Brown as if he was human with possible problems of his own," she said, and he sent her a quick, rather wary look as though she had caught him out in an unintentional slip.

"Well, if one accepts the fact that your patron is unlikely to be the equivalent of a computer, one must,

I suppose, allow him a modicum of natural feelings—but enough of Mr. Brown. Having exchanged a few home truths on the matter of my dubious attentions I insist upon spending the rest of the day in amicable harmony and the hope of furthering my private aims, despite your doubts," he said, reverting firmly to his more usual manner and holding out a hand for her empty glass.

She thought it wiser not to pursue the ambiguous subject of his private aims by asking awkward questions, but she hoped very much for a return of yesterday's felicity and knew in her heart that she no longer had any wish to withstand his persuasions.

There were few opportunities, however, for recapturing the mood of yesterday. Rain persisted steadily through the afternoon, putting paid to Robert's original plan for a trip to the coast and a bathe.

Robert had lighted a small fire in the parlour to offset the gloom of the afternoon, although it was warm enough, and Victoria was grateful for the cosiness and an illusion of continued intimacy, but she could not quite recapture the magic of yesterday which had ended so fittingly with moonlight and the miracle of a shooting star. Robert, too, seemed in no hurry to renew his attentions or, perhaps, he was too wise to try to recall a mood that was already in the past and, although he still contrived to coax responses from her with a skill she was as yet too inexperienced to appreciate, he made no move to kiss her or even to touch her.

Kate, expected back that evening, had been vague about her train and said she would take a taxi up from the station, but Victoria, as time went on, found she had an ear alert for the sounds of arrival distracting her attention from Robert, and when Elspeth brought in the tea, delivering Timmy at the same time, she was grateful for the chance to revert to her more customary place in the household before Kate returned.

Robert watched her with amusement, admiring the determination with which she sought to ignore the subtle implications of the past two days, knowing with increasing tenderness that however in the future she might regret her weakness in accepting his overtures, she would never again be able to whip up that old animosity with quite such uncaring ease.

When tea was finished he obligingly joined in the games Victoria devised for Timmy, sitting on the floor and devoting his attention entirely to his godson. Although the boy received his efforts with satisfaction, his response was a little wary. To him the week-end had not only been a bitter disappointment but filled with uneasy doubts. The godfather so long admired and taken for granted had in his mother's absence seemed different and rather like a stranger in a grown-up sort of way, and even his dear Toria had become grown-up too and had secrets with his Uncle Rab and not with him. He wished that Uncle John was his godfather, for, though not so entertaining as Uncle Rab, he never laughed at you or made funny jokes you couldn't understand and he was always exactly the same. He was thinking all these things as they played Snakes and Ladders, a game he had been newly introduced to and hadn't quite got the hang of, and Robert chose that moment to point out that he had cheated.

"What's cheated?" he demanded, sounding immediately truculent, for he knew very well it was something bad, even if he didn't grasp the implication. Robert explained patiently, giving demonstrations with the counters, making a joke about the snakes which you must always come down because they were slippery so that it was cheating to try to go up them.

Timmy listened unsmilingly, then firmly announced that if he wanted to go up a snake he would, so there!

"In that case nobody would play with you, so you'd have to play by yourself," his godfather retorted good-naturedly, and the boy's face began to grow scarlet. Victoria, knowing the signs, tried hastily to find excuses for him, but she was too late.

"Don't care, don't care! Who wants to play with silly old snakes, anyway? *You're* a snake, Uncle Rab—a big, ugly, slippery snake, and I hate you!" he shouted, snatching up the board with its remaining counters and hurling them at Robert.

"Now this is where you learn your lesson, young man," Robert exclaimed, getting to his feet and picking up the child in one swift movement. He sat down in the nearest chair with the boy across his knee and Timmy let out such a roar that Victoria clapped her hands to her ears. He was making so much noise that none of them heard a car draw up outside, but his screams must have sounded alarming to Kate, for she did not wait to pay off the taxi but ran into the house and flung open the door of the parlour just as Robert brought his hand down on the child's wriggling bottom.

"For heaven's sake! What's going on?" she demanded breathlessly, and at the sound of her voice, Timmy twisted out of his godfather's grasp and flung himself upon her, his bellows changing to gulping sobs.

"Oh, dear, oh dear! What a moment to pick for a welcomed return to the bosom of your family," Robert observed, getting to his feet. "I'm afraid you've caught me in the act of administering a long-delayed spanking to your son and heir."

If Kate heard him she was too concerned with soothing her child to pay very much heed. She was on her knees, with her arms tight round him, trying to elucidate the flood of grievances which poured from him, and her eyes, meeting Victoria's, were reproachful.

"What have you been doing to him?" she demanded. "He's feverish and probably has a chill."

"The feverish appearance is due to temper, not a chill, dear Kate," Robert interposed, with that suggestion of amused tolerance for human unreason which he could assume so devastatingly at times, and Kate looked at him angrily.

"Then you've probably upset him. If I'd known you were thinking of coming down for the day I'd have come back in the morning and none of this would have happened," she replied with rather a sweeping disregard for cause and effect, and Robert grinned.

"Well, I suppose it's possible you might have averted trouble, but it would have been a shame to cut your holiday short before you'd even got started. I came down on Friday," he said quite gently, and she disengaged Timmy's clinging hands and got slowly to her feet.

"You mean you've spent the week-end here?" she said, her voice sounding tight and unfamiliar.

"Yes, do you mind? I wasn't to know, of course, that you wouldn't be here, but Victoria kindly made me welcome."

"I'm sure she did. It's even possible she made the suggestion herself. She's been concerned at your absence for some little time," Kate snapped.

"Has she indeed?" said Robert with interest, but made no attempt to corroborate or otherwise, and Victoria, convinced now that Kate's feelings for her cousin went only too plainly rather deeper than friendship, experienced an unreasoning sense of guilt as if she had indeed, been responsible for engineering the visit. This was no time, however, for denials, with Robert standing there, quite undisturbed, and clearly rather enjoying the situation.

"I'm sorry you should think that, Kate," she said in a cool little voice. "I had no more idea than you of Robert's intentions, but since he looks on this as his home and seldom does give notice of his arrival, it never occurred to me to refuse him a bed."

She was aware that Robert's eyes were resting on his cousin with a rather enigmatical expression and Kate coloured faintly as if conscious that in the heat of the moment brought about by matronly concern she had spoken without her usual logical calm. She smiled a little ruefully at Victoria.

"Of course it didn't," she said. "I'm afraid I spoke without thinking. All the same, Robert should have known better."

"What! Knocked up the local at that hour of night to take me in in case the neighbours talked?" Robert exclaimed, and Victoria felt greatly relieved when Elspeth, appearing in the doorway to welcome Kate back, arrived in time to catch his remark and said in her nursery voice, and with a significant broadening of accent:

"You'll surely no be fashin' yoursel' with gossiping tongues after all this time, Mrs. Allen. There's many a week-end Mr. Rab visited here, with only mysel' to presairve the proprieties, and no talk ever came out of that, to my sairtain knowledge."

"That was different. I'm a widow with a child and old enough to ignore the conventions," Kate replied, but she sounded as if she knew it to be a weak defence, and Elspeth sniffed.

"Widows are no less immune from gossip as far as I know, and you're no' so old that a man wouldna look at you twice," she retorted tartly, "but let me take this laddie off to his bed now he's stopped his bawling and you sit down and rest yourself until he's ready to be tucked up. Run along, Timmy, your mammy's back safe and sound and she'll be up in a wee while to read you a story."

Robert, taking the hint, was already filling glasses for the evening aperitif and Timmy allowed himself to be led away without protest. Victoria, anxious not only to fulfil her duties but to leave the two cousins to settle their differences without being hampered by her presence, ran up the little corner staircase as a short cut to the nursery and hoped that Kate's homecoming hadn't been spoiled by such an explosive reception.

"That's better," Robert said as Kate took off her hat, tossing it carelessly on to the floor, and relaxed in a deep chair with her drink. "I can appreciate that arriving at such an unpropitious moment you were naturally thrown off balance, but you were acting a little out of character, don't you think?"

"No, I don't. I'll admit that in the heat of the moment I probably said more than was wise, but I'm concerned for that child's reputation so long as I'm responsible for her, and you should have had more sense than to invite trouble with the authorities."

"What authorities? I'm not aware that one requires a licence for week-end visiting."

"Oh, don't be so deliberately aggravating! You know very well I was alluding to the solicitors and their charges upon my responsibility. What do you suppose their reaction will be when news of this innocent week-end reaches them?"

"Not so obvious as yours, one must hope. In any case

there's no reason to suppose your absence from home would be unduly noticed."

"I daresay not, since the girl isn't without tact and a sense of discretion—still, I can hardly tell her not to mention it when she writes without giving her ideas she's better without."

"Then you will have to keep your fingers crossed and rely on that sense of discretion, won't you?" he replied, sounding, she thought, reprehensibly unconcerned.

"You don't seem to realise how tricky this situation could be," she said rather sharply. "It's not a question of morality or even of outdated conventions, but the peculiar conditions laid down by Mr. Brown. Any minute Victoria could be removed from my care and no reasons given. Old Mr. Chapple made it very plain at the time that a concession had been made in the matter of temporary employment only so long as I complied with certain provisos. It puts me in a very awkward position."

"Not so awkward as that of poor Victoria Mary should your forebodings come to pass," he retorted with rather unseemly levity, and she glanced up at him, frowning.

"Oh, you're in one of your tiresome moods!" she exclaimed crossly. "I've no doubt the whole thing strikes you as a trivial storm in a teacup, which it well may be, but at least you might consider Victoria's point of view. She's happy here with a pleasant illusion of home, and wouldn't take at all kindly to being uprooted again for lack of a little forethought."

"All of which is unlikely to occur for such far-fetched reasons, but even if it did—" he said, and stopped.

"Yes? Even if it did?"

"It would scarcely be the end of the road for Victoria, only for Mr. Brown," he concluded softly, and she glanced at him suspiciously.

"What do you mean by that ambiguous remark?" she asked, and went on without waiting for an answer: "Incidentally, I've a bone to pick with you—quite a large bone in view of this surprise visit."

"What have I done now to flaunt the conventions, or is it merely a matter of personal annoyance?"

"Nothing personal as far as I'm concerned, but I happened to run into Irene in London, looking very glamorous and expensive and bursting with well-bred curiosity about your latest conquest."

"What on earth are you talking about?"

"Only that she apparently happened to meet you one day coming out of Flora's where you used to spend such a fortune on flowers for her and had the inquisitiveness to go inside and make enquiries. They were most discreet, of course, and mentioned no names, but the address you had written out was still lying on the counter, and since it was only too familiar to Irene, it set her thinking."

"And her thoughts presumably fixed on you?"

"Oh, no. Irene may have been piqued by our long friendship, but she never considered me worth a jealous pang—besides, the name of the mysterious recipient of five dozen highly-priced roses was plainly written above the address and, being a new one to Irene, set her agog with speculation."

"Very likely, since women are never content to relinquish old claims, but it's scarcely a matter of much moment, is it?"

"Perhaps you've forgotten," Kate said rather deliberately after a glance at his face, "that Victoria received five dozen roses from Mr. Brown on her birthday, but only a card from you."

"Well, what of it?" Robert retorted, and turned to replenish his glass so that she had no means of reading anything from his expression.

"What of it? Well, surely there must be an explanation, unless you were just amusing yourself at her expense, which wouldn't have been very nice. What *are* you up to, Rob? Flowers purporting to come from a stranger you've always rather ridiculed, and now picking the one week-end to appear yourself, when I'm conveniently out of the way."

"That was just the luck of the draw—I'd really no idea you were in London," he answered casually. "As for the flowers, it seemed a pity not to give Mr. Brown's image a boost by crediting him with something warmer than the dictates of cold charity."

All at once Kate was angry. She knew from past experience that she would learn nothing from Robert by calling him to account, but she had a sudden clear picture of the soft radiance lighting up Victoria's face as she looked down at the roses in her arms and said wonderingly. "They've crowned my whole day . . ." and suddenly itched to pick a quarrel with him. "Cold charity is at least more honest than an attempt to bamboozle an unsuspecting innocent for one's private amusement," she snapped at him. "You must have a peculiar sense of humour, Robert, if playing tricks of this sort affords you entertainment."

"I think," he replied with the sudden icy politeness of a stranger, "we won't pursue this subject any further. I have nothing to say that would satisfy you at this juncture, neither am I prepared to justify my actions. However, I would strongly advise you to keep your knowledge to yourself unless you're out to make trouble."

"I wouldn't dream of reducing that bright bubble of happiness to the ugly reality of an ill-timed jest for my own satisfaction, but watch your step, my dear. It isn't wise to tread on dreams lightly and the young have a right to theirs however foolish they may seem to others," Kate said, and jumped, spilling her drink on her smart new suit as Victoria's voice said from the bottom of the staircase:

"Thank you, Kate, but I'd rather know. It's much more humiliating to be bolstered up with fairy tales to save one's pride than to face the fact that one has been made a fool of."

There was an instant of shocked silence. Kate dabbed ineffectually at the stain on her skirt while she sought vainly for the right words: Robert, standing by the fireplace, put his half-empty glass down on the mantelshelf, creating a staccato sharpness of sound, but otherwise did not move, and Victoria remained where she was at the foot of the stairs. Her face was rather white, its planes and angles sharply accentuated giving her a curiously fragile look, but she held herself very erect with an odd kind of stillness which was strangely moving.

"How much have you heard?" Kate asked at last realizing the futility of trying to cover up with soothing improvisations.

"Oh, everything, I think," Victoria answered still in those cool, unhurried tones. "I listened, you know. I listened quite deliberately. I was coming down to tell you Timmy was ready to be tucked up and I heard you reproving Robert for coming down this week-end and I thought he might say something which would give me a clue to—to certain things I wanted to know. Then you sidetracked him with your discovery about the roses, so I just sat at the top of the stairs till you had both finished. As you said yourself, Kate, it wasn't a very nice trick to play, knowing how much I've always hoped for some sign of interest from Mr. Brown, but I suppose I was fair game. Robert, I realise now, is fond of playing tricks to pass the time, but I won't be had again. Will you go up to Timmy? He's looking forward to his bedtime story."

Robert still said nothing, and Kate got slowly to her feet, uncertain whether it was best to leave them alone, or try to minimise the consequences of a crisis she had unwittingly brought about.

"Victoria . . ." she began hesitantly as she crossed the room ". . . . it's no use saying I'm sorry you overheard our conversation, but you mustn't think you were being made a fool of. I'm sure there's a perfectly good explanation for Robert's odd behaviour, so don't . . ." She tailed off rather lamely and Victoria prompted politely: "Don't what?"

"Nothing. There's nothing I can possibly advise in the circumstances. I'll be in the nursery if you want me, but I won't come down till I'm called," Kate replied, adding over her shoulder as she passed Victoria at the foot of the stairs: "And you'd better make your excuses good, Robert, if you want to keep your newly-won advantage."

Robert stooped with leisurely deliberation to throw another log on the fire.

"Well . . ." he said at last as Victoria did not move, ". . . hadn't you better come and sit down? There's no point in us shouting abuse at one another across the width of the room."

"I haven't been shouting, and I see no reason why you should need the support of abuse," she replied with that strange, unnatural composure, and he frowned, impatient of his careless phrasing.

"Quite right. I was presuming, I'm afraid, on experience of other occasions when sparring matches between us took on rather a flavour of prep-school retaliation," he said, deliberately using the teasing intonation which used to rile her in the past, hoping to goad her into an outburst which would relieve her feelings.

"Yes, well . . ." she said a little absently as if the past no longer greatly mattered, "I daresay I was easy meat, not being at all experienced in the art of repartee, but you hadn't much in the way of opposition to sharpen your wits on, had you?"

"You think not? Well, Victoria Mary, it may please you to know that I found your repartee exhilarating and by no means adolescent, if that's what you were implying," he answered, still with that light raillery, but she looked at him with grave consideration, then said bleakly:

"It doesn't please me at all. It only points an obvious truth that I was a convenient butt to provide entertainment for your idle moments."

His manner underwent a subtle change and when next he spoke it was with the measured coolness he employed in court and his face became the cold, clever mask she had first known and disliked.

"If that's what you think, you can hardly absolve yourself entirely," he retorted. "You would have been willing enough, I fancy, to come to terms with me had I pressed my advantage this week-end, despite these unflattering opinions, On second thoughts, perhaps I was too forbearing and merely disappointed you."

He regretted his words as soon as he saw the colour flooding her cheeks and her slender body seeming to shrink from an unexpected blow, but at least, he reflected wryly, he had succeeded in breaking through that alarming composure.

"That of course is what I should have expected from you," she countered swiftly, and there was already a hint of tears in her voice. "All right, then! I'm too honest

114

or too silly to deny that I was willing to be made love to because I thought . . well, it doesn't matter now what I thought, but you at least might have had the decency to leave me my illusions . . . to pretend, even though it was only make-believe, that you had found me p-pleasing."

She was crying now, quite unaware of it, and he gave a sharp exclamation and crossed the room in two strides to take her by the shoulders.

"You foolish, pig-headed little idiot! What do you suppose I was about if I didn't find you pleasing?" he exclaimed, shaking her quite hard. "I may have made a mess of the whole damned business, but I wasn't scheming to seduce you, whatever you may think now."

"I don't know what to think," she said on a note of distraction, and stood very still, weeping on his shoulder for a snatched moment of comfort, then tried to pull away from him.

"No, you don't," he said, tightening his grip. "Not until we get this nonsense sorted out. Will you listen, now, while I plead my case?"

She nodded.

"You'll remember we talked of a time that would be ripe for disenchantment," he began, leading her to the fire and putting her gently into a chair. "I don't think that time is quite yet, but I'll have to take a chance on being premature and crave your indulgence."

She had stopped crying and was listening to him politely but without much comprehension, and he realised he had made an error in trying to pave the way by wrapping his intentions in a semblance of make-believe when she said in a tired voice:

"You don't have to go on pandering to my adolescent dream-world. I'm quite capable of distinguishing between fantasy and reality, even though I still sometimes like to make images."

"I'm sure you are. Very well, I won't waste time any longer trying for the delicate approach. Will you marry me, Victoria Mary Hayes, and try to overcome that aversion for browbeating barristers?"

He had in sheer self-defence dropped back into flippancy to cloak a proposal which might come as something of a shock, but he was unprepared for the naked pain which suddenly darkened her eyes or the swift dismay with which she sprang to her feet.

"That was quite unnecessary, Robert," she said, and her voice was now completely steady and devoid of tears. "Whatever the unlucky results of this week-end, there's no occasion to make things worse with gentlemanly offers of rectitude."

"Good God!" he exclaimed, uncertain at that moment whether to laugh or be angry. "Where on earth do you get such phrases from? I can assure you that gentlemanly offers of rectitude wouldn't in my opinion be any sort of foundation for a successful marriage, or even as the price of seduction, so don't go weaving more fantasies to confuse the issue."

"I'm sorry you should think so poorly of my efforts to be practical. I was merely trying to relieve you of a misplaced sense of duty, and there's nothing particularly fanciful in that," she said, and he regarded her in thoughtful silence for a moment, cursing the impulse which had led him to speak against his better judgment, and wondering how best to deal with an intelligence temporarily closed to reason.

"You have a most curious trick of relapsing into slightly pompous pedantry on certain occasions," he observed, hoping to give her time to readjust her ideas, but she looked at him as if he had been guilty of some trivial irrelevance and replied without humour:

"Then I must have caught the trick from you. After all, I haven't had much chance since coming to Farthings of associating with men of my own age and habits of speech, have I?"

"All right, you've made your point," Robert said, and the bite was back in his voice. "I realise that it could be said that I've taken advantage of your rather unique situation, but there's no need to throw it in my face. It seems I've misjudged both the moment and your own rather misleading behaviour, so we'll shelve your answer until a more propitious time."

"My answer?"

"Perhaps you've already forgotten that little item, or

116

wasn't it important? Never mind, the time wasn't ripe, so we'll let that pass, but there's one thing I *would* like to know. Was I only deceiving myself by imagining a change of heart in you?" His voice softened as he asked the question, the ghost of that tender smile touching his lips, and for a moment Victoria wavered. It would be so easy to abandon resistance and shut one's eyes both to disillusioning reality and to the pricklings of conscience, but because her conscience had never been entirely easy in regard to Kate, she could only answer him indirectly by blurting out as she had once before:

"And what of Kate?"

"Kate?" He frowned impatiently. "Oh yes, Kate . . . It was a pity you had to find out about those roses, but if you hadn't succumbed to temptation and eavesdropped on our conversation, you'd have been none the wiser, so don't blame poor Kate for giving the show away."

She, in turn, supposed him to have purposely sidetracked her, but the casual mention of that most bitter hurt to her pride successfully silenced any qualms of conscience in regard to Kate.

"Why?" she asked. "Why did you have to play such a pointless practical joke on me? To make fun of me by letting me believe in something that wasn't true was not only stupid but heartless."

"Stupid, possibly, but not intentionally heartless," he replied, but there was little of warmth in his voice now, only a cool note of tolerance as if he was humouring an unreasonable child and, like a child, she stamped her foot at him.

"That's no excuse and no answer either," she flashed out. "If I could understand what prompted you — but I can't."

"Can't you? Well, no, how should you? Let's say, then, that it seemed a pity not to endow unimaginative Mr. Brown with a little fictional awareness of his more tender obligations in view of past omissions, and you must admit, Victoria Mary, that true or false, the result was fully justified."

"Don't go on addressing me in that silly manner as if my names as well as my greenness amused you," she snapped back, sounding, at last, more like her usual self. "Nothing's justified as it's turned out, unless you count your success in making a fool of me, and for that I can't forgive you."

"No, I suppose not," he said, sounding suddenly tired and not very interested. "Well, I'll just have to make the best of it, won't I?"

"Is that all you care?" she asked, but if he caught the tentative plea for assurance in her voice he ignored it.

"You're not, I fancy, in the right mood to assess degrees of emotion, so the answer had better be yes, I care to the extent of not wishing to hurt you unnecessarily, but I'm too old and seasoned not to have learned acceptance. You might with good effect apply a little of the same philosophy to your own situation when you've got over your disappointment regarding Mr. Brown. There are worse things in life than the loss of one's youthful illusions."

"None of which explains anything," she protested, striving to capture a shred of dignity. "It's very easy to wrap things up in a lot of high-sounding nonsense that doesn't mean a thing, but you owe me more than that, Robert. So far, you've offered me nothing definite to come to terms with."

"I've offered you marriage, but perhaps you don't consider that definite enough," he replied quite gently.

"But that," she countered quickly before her resistance could be further weakened, "was probably a hoax. It was all a hoax, wasn't it? The roses, the surprise weekend, even the moonlight and the shooting star — everything laid on to lend enchantment where none existed."

He made a small involuntary movement towards her then thrust his hands in his trouser pockets and leaned back against the mantelshelf.

"You must, of course, draw your own conclusions about that," he said with cool deliberation. "I'm not prepared to make palatable concessions as a sop to hurt feelings. You must take me as you find me, my dear, or not at all."

"Then," she replied with a studied politeness which she hoped would match his own coolness, "it will have to be not at all, if you really need an answer. I must apologise, Robert, for being so dumb that I mistook fantasy for fact, but it won't occur again. I'll go up and tell

Kate she can come down now. It must be nearly supper time."

She turned as she finished speaking and crossed the room to escape up the staircase which had provided such disastrous facilities for eavesdropping, and Robert watched her go, but made no attempt to call her back. When, a few minutes later, Kate came down, he was already collecting his personal possessions which lay scattered about the room and paused only to say:

"I'll pour you a drink in a moment, Kate, then I'll go upstairs and get packed."

"But you don't need to do that yet," she said, switching on lights and drawing curtains to shut out the depressing view of the lingering daylight. "You never do leave till late on Sundays."

"There are Sundays and Sundays, and I won't stay for your cold collation if you don't mind," he replied, and she glanced quickly at his face, then as quickly away.

"Oh, dear! Didn't you straighten things out?" she said, and sounded faintly exasperated. She had not expected to return to her home to find complications leading to strained relationships and no one very interested in how she herself had spent the week-end.

"Quite the opposite. Confusion was only piled upon confusion," he replied, pouring her a drink, and his voice held such a touch of bitterness that her eyes became thoughtful.

"Well," she said, "leaving aside the question of whether or not your visit was wise, I'll confess I find your prank with the roses a little hard to take. How did you explain that away to Victoria?"

"I didn't, neither am I going to explain it to you. You will just have to write it off as an eccentricity and blame that peculiar sense of humour of which you accused me earlier."

"And is that all the satisfaction you afforded Victoria? I wonder she didn't up and dot you one!"

He smiled then, but his eyes were a little sad as he handed her the drink he had poured for her.

"It would possibly have saved a lot of heartburning if she had," he replied, "but Miss Victoria Mary Hayes

119

showed a remarkable restraint for the most part and I — well, I probably took up the wrong attitude and discovered it too late to start afresh."

"Are you serious, Rob?" she asked him curiously, not very sure what answer she wanted him to make, and he raised one eyebrow with that trick he had when he chose to be uncommunicative.

"I'm perfectly serious in regretting my own short-comings," he replied, "and will you now, please, revert to your usual tactful self and forbear to plague me with awkward questions?"

"No, I will not," she retorted with spirit. "I'm very fond of you, Rob, and grateful for all that you do to make life pleasant for Timmy and me, but I have a responsibility to the girls I employ and Victoria in particular with all those tiresome provisos I've had to comply with. She's not, thank heavens, a silly young miss with her head full of romantic nonsense, but she's had little chance to be courted and admired in the usual way. You, after all, are a very attractive man when you set out to charm, and I wouldn't like to think you've embarked on making a conquest just for the sake of amusement. There! Tell me to mind my own business if you like, but don't be surprised if I claim the rights of an old friend, to say nothing of a relation."

"A very distant one — just sufficiently connected to make our association respectable," he said with a grin. "Are you by any chance asking my intentions, sweet Kate?"

"Yes, I think I am. I think I hope that you *are* serious, for it's high time you settled down with someone who could make you happy. You've waited too long as a result of overdone caution. Irene was simply typical of her own set and upbringing and the only mistake you made was in thinking you could change her. But you're older now, and possibly not so exacting in your demands for perfection. Whether Victoria is old enough or experienced enough to satisfy you, I wouldn't know, but the pernickety Mr. Brown has certainly seen to it that there's been small chance of her developing a taste for riotous living, so at least you'd be spared a repetition of the Irene fiasco.

There — I've said my piece, and if you don't like it you'll just have to lump it!"

"Well, that was quite a speech, Cousin Kate," he said, sounding amused and slightly surprised. "I must say I admire the temerity with which you stick to your guns, and I'll reward it this much to relieve your doubts. I asked Victoria to marry me just now, so you can put your mind at rest concerning my intentions. Unfortunately she didn't take the same view, dismissing my proposal either as a gentlemanly offer to offset gossip or a hoax on the same lines as that unfortunate affair of the roses."

"So she turned you down. Well, I can't say I'm surprised, all things considered. Why on earth, if you were building up to a romantic scene, didn't you send your wretched floral offering from yourself instead of foisting them on to Mr. Brown, who for all we know, is still trying to work out how the mistake occurred?"

"Now that, as they say, is another story, and not one that I'm prepared to embark upon. You will, I hope, Kate, be discreet if Victoria sees fit to confide in you— no well-intentioned persuasions on my behalf, please. This is something she will have to work out for herself. Now, I really must get my things together and be off before the poor child comes down for supper, bracing herself to sit through an embarrassing meal as if nothing had happened."

"Rob . . ." Kate said, catching at his sleeve when he kissed her quickly in passing, ". . . won't you . . . wouldn't you like to . . . ? I can tell Elspeth to put supper back and retire upstairs to my room."

"No, I wouldn't like, dear Kate. The moment isn't propitious for the recapturing of magic and poor Victoria's dream world has taken a hard knock. I won't come down here again unless you send for me, so I'll say goodbye now and slip away when the coast is clear," he said, and left her, instinctively avoiding the habitual short cut to the bedrooms provided by the corner staircase.

CHAPTER EIGHT

BUT Victoria did no confiding and Kate, remembering that disconcerting trick of cool withdrawal, if disappointed, was unsurprised. Robert, she thought had not allowed for a maturity of mind which the years of enforced dependence had fostered early.

When they met at supper that Sunday evening, it had been Kate who appeared awkward and at a loss for conversation. Victoria might have wept in the privacy of her room, but she was composed enough at the supper-table and if she ate little, she gave no other sign of being distressed, relieved no doubt by Robert's decision to absent himself. Kate found herself answering polite questions and giving dutiful accounts of her doings in London as if it were she who were required to be set at ease, and although she tried once or twice to provide an opening for reciprocal confidences, she was neatly sidetracked. No mention was made of Robert's sudden departure or the extraordinary trick he had seen fit to play, but the next morning, Kate found the roses had been replaced with hastily picked oddments from the garden.

"What have you done with them?" she asked casually, wondering whether Victoria had, on a sentimental impulse, removed them all to her own room to brood over them in solitude, but felt snubbed when she was answered equally casually:

"I threw them away. They were beginning to drop."

"Oh, what a pity!" was all Kate could find to say. "They may have been dropping, but they weren't nearly dead."

"They were to me. I find I don't care for roses as much as I once did — they're an overrated luxury if you don't grow them yourself," Victoria said, and began to talk brightly of something else

As the days went on, a sense of unease troubled them both. It seemed to Kate that that unfortunate week-end had sparked off something which affected the whole household.

"I wish I'd never gone away that week-end. Nothing's been quite the same since," Kate confided in John Squires on one of her customary stops for a glass of sherry on her way home from the village.

"In what way?" he enquired cautiously. He had never alluded to Robert's visit during her absence but, quite apart from the fact that, like himself, she probably thought it unwise, he imagined she could well have been hurt by this show of interest in a younger woman.

"Oh, I don't know. Perhaps leaving home unsettled me. I'm not really cut out for the gay life and I've bought a lot of new clothes I could quite well do without."

"Haven't they been properly appreciated?"

"Oh, yes, Victoria is most approving and even Elspeth pays me a grudging compliment or two. It was she, as a matter of fact, who persuaded me into extravagance in the first place, but lately she's been a bit crotchety, as though she regretted departing from her native caution."

"And the attentive cousin — wasn't he impressed?"

"Robert? Well, there was scarcely time for him to notice new clothes. He went back before supper. There — well, there had been a little disagreement with Victoria over something and he thought it better not to stay late."

"I see. It might have been wiser if he hadn't stayed at all in the circumstances. Did you mind, Kate?"

"Not really," she answered evasively. "I did think at the time it might have caused awkwardness if it got to the ears of that tiresome Mr. Brown, but it was probably only due to a slight sense of guilt."

"Why on earth should you blame yourself?" he exclaimed angrily. "Farmer should have known better than to upset you with thoughtless behaviour."

"Oh, I don't really — only to the extent of having Victoria removed from my employment as a result of any carelessness on my part. You've no idea how fussy those pompous solicitors are, but Robert didn't upset me for that reason."

"Oh, I see." He did not enquire for the true reason, having no wish for his suspicions to be confirmed, but Kate, mistaking his reticence for censure of Robert, found herself on dangerous ground. He had not sworn her to secrecy in the matter of his rejected proposal, but she felt it was premature to discuss his prospects when so much lay unresolved.

"I don't think you do, John dear, but it wouldn't be fair to Robert to discuss his affairs at this juncture, so just forget my little burst of discontent," she said, and wished as she saw the familiar expression of patient resignation in his steady blue eyes that she could have sought his counsel and understanding for the doubts which still troubled her.

"This weather's enough to breed discontent in the hardiest of us," he replied, taking his cue and thankful for the never-failing excuse of the weather's vagaries, and she smiled at him gratefully.

"Yes, it is, isn't it?" she agreed, getting up reluctantly to go. "The week-end I was in London was so hot that I thought nostalgically of the country, and now this! Timmy, incidentally, hasn't been himself lately. I think he got a bit of a chill and hasn't shaken it off. I was sure he was running a temperature then, though Robert said it was only spleen."

"And Farmer was probably right," John said briskly. "We don't see eye to eye on many matters, but we do share the opinion that you fuss too much about the boy."

She was used to his plain speaking and respected his medical skill, but he had never before accused her quite so openly of maternal foolishness.

"But, John, he's all I have! I can't help being overanxious at times," she said, and stood looking at him a little helplessly with hurt brown eyes, but he became suddenly too impatient of the strictures which clouded his own situation to offer the usual soothing assurances.

"It's no fault of the child's that he's all you have," he retorted bluntly. "Being a born mother, you're simply suffering from frustration. You should marry again and have other children to keep you busy and happy in the way you were meant for."

"*Well!*" she said a little blankly, and found to her surprise that she was blushing. "If anyone but you had said that to me, John, I'd—"

"You'd what?"

"I've really no idea! I think I'd better return home before you offer me any more surprising advice."

"I could offer advice that might surprise but probably wouldn't please you," he said soberly, "so I won't risk our valuable friendship by being too outspoken. Do you want me to come up and run the rule over Timmy to prove your anxieties groundless?"

"Yes, if you would. I'm not really so anxious as all that, but it makes a nice excuse for your company. Besides, Victoria and I need cheering up," she said, and returned to Farthings feeling suddenly gay and indifferent to the weather, and rather pleased that she had spent more than she should on some becoming new clothes.

But if Kate contrived to ignore the discomforts of the rest of that chilly June, Victoria found the grey skies and perpetual drizzle a discouraging if fit complement to her own disturbance of mind. She became morbidly conscious of a sense of guilt. However trivial Robert's attentions had turned out to be, the fact remained that she had been ready and willing to receive them because for her he had ceased to be the enemy of old. She did not blame him now for having misled her or for that ridiculous proposal which she supposed was his way of offering amends, but taken all together with that pointless practical joke involving Mr. Brown, the whole sorry affair was reduced to bitterness.

"The courts will be rising soon," Kate said to her one day with apparent irrelevance, adding when Victoria looked politely enquiring but made no rejoinder: "Robert was going to spend part of the Long Vacation here, you know."

"Was he?"

"Yes, he was. He usually has until this year."

"Well, I suppose he's changed his plans. People do," Victoria replied, trying to sound rational and disinterested, but in Kate's over-sensitive ears she appeared to be offering a polite snub.

"Well, you needn't be so smug about it," Kate retorted sharply. "I've no doubt a change of plans suits you, but this is Robert's home when all's said and done, and it's a little hard that he should feel obliged to stop away in order not to upset a young girl I happen to employ."

"That," Victoria replied, sounding strained but still infuriatingly polite, "is surely an exaggeration. Robert, I imagine, would hardly consider the feelings of an employee if it interfered with his own convenience. Aren't you making rather a thing out of that unlucky week-end?"

"No," said Kate, seizing her opportunity when at last it offered with an uncharacteristic abandonment of reserve. "It's you who, I suspect, has magnified things out of all proportion. I can respect your effort to cover up hurt feelings with a show of indifference, but not this refusal to come to terms with yourself."

"Oh, I've done that," Victoria said quietly, her eyes grave and curiously wordly-wise, and Kate blurted out before she could stop herself:

"Are you in love with him, Victoria?"

"I don't think you should ask me that, Kate. I may have been silly and extremely green, but my feelings are my own business and quite unimportant."

Resentment began to stir in Kate. Although she could, in her rational moments, allow that everyone was entitled to privacy, it was humiliating to be put in one's place by a chit of a girl who, unintentionally or not, was causing so much trouble.

"Very well," she said, controlling an impulse to quarrel vulgarly by taking refuge instead in the authority of an employer, "you are, of course, entitled to keep your own counsel, but if, as you state, your feelings are unimportant, I would be glad if you didn't let them interfere with your obligations here at Farthings. Elspeth tells me you spend too much time in the kitchen asking vague questions about the past which she's in no position to answer and you seem to have temporarily lost your touch with Timmy. Children's attachments can, I know, be fickle and subject to change, but it would be a pity if he turned against his godfather for want of a little tact on your part."

Victoria had listened without interruption or protest, but her face had grown whiter and more sharply angled and she looked as she had that evening standing at the foot of the stairs saying so quietly that it was more humiliating to be bolstered up with fairy tales than to face the fact that one had been made a fool of. For a moment Kate felt

126

ashamed of resorting to cheap criticism to relieve her feeling, but before she could add a word of retraction, Victoria said in a voice which had lost its cool confidence and sounded bewildered and very young:

"Then it would be better if I went away. I—I'm sorry, Kate, if I've been the cause of — of any trouble, but Timmy will soon forget his resentment of Robert once I've gone. He was only jealous. I shall miss you, Kate, but it will be better this way."

Kate watched her with troubled eyes. She wanted to take the girl in her arms, to tell her the whole thing was a storm in a teacup and was best forgotten by both of them, but there was too much truth in Victoria's sad conclusions and, for her own sake, it might be wiser to make a break while there was still time to forget.

"Yes, perhaps it would," she said with a regretful sigh. "Not because I was finding fault, perhaps unfairly, but because I think it might be best for you. I shall miss you, too, very much, but it needn't be the end of friendship. You'll come back here one day for a visit."

"You said that in Switzerland when I thought Mr. Brown wouldn't agree — do you remember? Even if he won't, you said, you can at least come on a visit and we'll pick up the threads. How long ago it all seems," Victoria said, and thought as she had then that those sort of promises were usually doomed to be unfulfilled, but Kate frowned.

"Yes, I'd forgotten Mr. Brown. I'd better write and make tactful explanations and perhaps suggest some alternative plan to see you through the next few months."

"No, I'll write. A course at some commercial college would fill in the time nicely before the Trust is wound up, and the solicitors, at least, would see the sense in that and point out to Mr. Brown that I could hardly be expected to earn a respectable living without some sort of training. He should, of course, have thought of that long ago."

Victoria, having delivered her little speech with matter-of-fact finality, was gone before Kate could form any suitable reply, and she sat down limply in the nearest easy chair, feeling despondent and somehow at fault. She considered ringing up Robert to ask advice, but she knew him too well to expect interference in a situation which involved himself. He would find his own way of resolving his difficulties when and if the time came and, whether or not Victoria had been near to loving him before being shocked into apathy by that pointless deception, it would be better to allow her time to readjust in some other environment than stop on at Farthings with perpetual reminders of a spoiled dream.

She remembered now that it had been Robert who had casually acquainted her with the girl's whereabouts and suggested the possibility of arriving at some mutual agreement. He must, she supposed with slight surprise, have kept track of the child's progress through the years, owing to his irrational sense of responsibility at the outcome of the trial.

Had Robert been merely curious to see how she had turned out, thanks to a benefactor who must have shared something of his own disquiet, or had he more definite plans which he hoped would mature given the appropriate environment and careful handling? And why, thought Kate with a fresh renewal of exasperated curiosity, when he was so nearly within reach of his goal, had he chosen to play a trick which, if discovered, could only result in wreckage? As it was, she had no doubts that the watchful Mr. Brown would be prompt in removing his protegée to more suitable quarters, and since it was only too likely that Robert's name had appeared with increasing regularity in Victoria's duty letters, it would not be difficult to arrive at a reason for her sudden request to leave. Robert was too well known in legal circles to escape censure should her letters have been indiscreet and one thing could lead to another . . .

The solicitors' reply to the letter Victoria had written about her plans was unexpected and far from helpful. Mr. Brown, they informed Victoria, was entirely satisfied with the present arrangement and saw no reason to make any changes, providing that Mrs. Allen was still willing to offer employment. They trusted that Miss Hayes was not being so inconsiderate at this late date as to indulge in girlish fancies, and remained hers faithfully.

"Girlish fancies indeed!" she exclaimed indignantly, shaking back her hair like a startled pony. Kate had been watching her across the breakfast table as she read the brief communication and gave a sympathetic smile.

"Yes, I've heard too," she said, meeting Victoria's outraged gaze with some wryness. "It looks as though we'll have to make the best of it, doesn't it?"

"You could always write and say you've sacked me. Even Mr. Brown could hardly insist on my remaining here in that case," Victoria replied, and Kate sighed.

"Probably not, but since the decision was yours and not mine, the question of sacking doesn't arise," she said briefly.

"But you agreed. You thought it was best in the circumstances. You could say with perfect truth that you found me unsatisfactory."

"I could, but I haven't. I thought it best only for your own sake, but as you evidently didn't see fit to explain your reasons for wanting to leave, you can't blame your Mr. Brown for not taking you seriously."

"It should have been sufficient that the arrangement didn't suit me. I'm not a child any longer to be dismissed as inconsequent and tiresome. Surely they must realise that I've rights which weren't in existence when the Trust was drawn up. If you can marry at eighteen without the consent of parents, and vote and be allowed H.P., there's no power that can stop you ordering your own life at twenty."

"No, there isn't," Kate admitted. "Still, I suppose one can't entirely rule out one's obligations. Your Mr. Brown may be a crank and a bit of a despot, but he's entitled to expect some return for his generosity. Well, it looks as if you'll have to submit with a good grace to stopping on here for a time. I can't in all honesty sack you to force a different decision and I don't suppose Mr. Brown or the lawyers would know what on earth to do with you if I did."

"No, I suppose they wouldn't. Oh, well, I'm sorry if you're stuck with me after all. Perhaps I should have made my reasons rather plainer," Victoria said, sounding flippant but looking as if she wanted to cry, and Kate's eyes grew soft. So the child hadn't played her strongest card and alleged unwelcome masculine attentions.

"Perhaps you should—" she said gently, "—if, that is, you think you were being taken advantage of."

Victoria lowered her lashes but did not quite succeed in hiding the brightness of tears.

"I try not to think at all," she replied, keeping her voice quite steady. "I was green and gullible and took too much for granted, I expect. If it hadn't been for that practical joke I might even have taken Robert seriously, so perhaps it's all worked out for the best."

"But, Victoria—"

"Don't try to explain things away with feeble excuses out of loyalty, Kate. I can guess that your own feelings were no less sore than mine, but I'm out of your way now —if I ever was in it."

"What on earth are you talking about? Is it possible that—"

"Can I speak to you a moment, Mrs. Allen?" said Elspeth's voice from the doorway. "If Miss Toria is leaving us shortly, you'd do well to be thinking of a replacement. I'm no' so young that I can take over Timmy for more than a wee while, so you'd best get out an advertisement for the local paper. A daily girl might suit us better than someone living in." She spoke as if Victoria were not present, and Kate frowned. The implied rebuke was no less annoying than the untimely interruption.

"Miss Toria isn't leaving us, after all, so there's no need for you to fuss," she said a little shortly. "You should know, in any case, that I'd not expect you to add Timmy to your other commitments."

"Verra guid," said Elspeth primly, pulling down the corners of her mouth and registering her displeasure by reverting to the well-trained servant whose opinions were neither asked for nor heeded. As she turned to leave the room, however, she added with the habit of long privilege: "You'll no' throw dust in my eyes, missus, by reminding me of my poseetion. There's a deal of nonsense goes on in this hoose that a mite of common sense would clear up without setting us all at odds."

130

"Oh, dear!" said Kate as the door closed behind her. "Now I've offended her. What were we saying, Victoria? I've an idea we were interrupted at a rather crucial moment."

"Nothing of any importance," Victoria answered. "I'd got rather tangled up with a lot of foolish thoughts as a result of Mr. Brown's refusal to play ball, but if you really want me to stay, Kate, that's all that matters. Let's forget the whole thing."

"Very well," Kate replied a shade stiffly, conscious of being gently put in her place, but she did not find as the days went on that it was easy to dismiss the matter so lightly. She was troubled not only by the girl's air of withdrawal, but the slight sense of strain which seemed to have crept into their pleasant relationship.

"It's a ridiculous situation," she complained to John Squires on one of his hurried visits. "I've no desire to get rid of Victoria, but I think she's beginning to feel she's here on sufferance thanks to the unco-operativeness of this tiresome Mr. Brown. Timmy seems to have forgotten his temporary resentment, which is something to be thankful for, I suppose, but Elspeth's particularly crotchety these days, and Robert keeps away."

"And that, of course, is the reason for your disquiet, my dear," John said with some dryness, and she looked at him in surprise.

"Are you implying that I'm jealous?"

"Well, aren't you? I have no means of knowing what, if any, understanding lies between you and Farmer, but you've regarded him as your special property for so long that it's only natural to be a little piqued."

"You have no earthly right to take me to task — to suggest motives that you can't possibly be sure of. You'll be accusing me next of being Robert's mistress and resenting the attractions of a younger woman!" Kate cried, but he had smothered his own feeling for too long to choose his next words with care.

"If that should, by any chance, be true, I would be the last to blame you," he said, refusing to raise his voice to match hers. "You are a young woman still, with healthy desires and appetites that should not be denied, but you'll

131

need more than that to satisfy you later on. You'll need marriage and children and the security of a legitimised union as you grow older, and it's time we, both of us, took stock."

Kate stared at him speechless for a moment while she sought vainly for the remnants of her old composure.

"Your tolerance is as insulting as your well-worn advice," she flung back at him then. "I suppose you'd be complacent enough to offer to supply all these things and kindly overlook any little lapse on my part."

"Hush, my poor, angry dear, don't throw my ill-expressed intentions back in my face. Whatever you may or may not have been to Robert Farmer has no bearing on my own feelings. I would have you, Kate, on any terms if I thought I could make you happy," he said, his blue eyes suddenly a little shy, and she burst into tears.

"Oh, go away . . . go away!" she wept, touched and exasperated at the same time, and because it had been too long since he had learnt to deal persuasively with a weeping woman he got up at once and took his leave of her. He had scarcely reached his car, however, when he was confronted by Victoria, who demanded indignantly to know what was the matter with him.

"Nothing that concerns you," he replied with unusual asperity, but she refused to be snubbed.

"Then you shouldn't quarrel with all the windows wide open," she retorted. "Why couldn't you take poor Kate in your arms and knock some sense into her instead of slinking off as if you'd put both feet in it?"

"I may very well have put both feet in it, but I wasn't aware of slinking off," he replied with the ghost of a smile. "Were you listening under the window, young woman?"

"Of course not, but I couldn't help hearing when Kate started to shout. Why do you let yourself be used just as a safety valve?"

"It's not a bad thing to one's credit if it eases the mind, and it's scarcely becoming in you to take me to task in the circumstances. Whatever Farmer's intentions may have been, Kate was happy enough in their association until you came."

She stared up at him, her eyes suddenly clouded with

the old doubts, and when she spoke her voice had lost its assurance.

"Do you think she's in love with him, John?" she asked, and he gave a little shrug.

"I don't know. It's always possible that the situation suited them both so long as there was no need to make decisions, but women can be possessive, even if they're not in love, and it can't have been very pleasant for Kate to have to acknowledge a shifting interest under her very nose. You should think of your own part in the affair, Victoria, before you accuse me of being chicken-hearted."

She went a little white, but her eyes were steady.

"Yes, I suppose I deserved that, but you don't know the ins and outs of that business," she replied. "I should have kept my head and written off the fruits of that weekend for what they were, instead of—"

"Instead of what, my child?"

"Oh, not what you were thinking. I didn't jump into bed with Robert, neither, to be honest, did he ask me to."

"It wasn't what I was thinking at all. You were going to say, I fancy, instead of falling in love with him," John replied gently, and her eyes filled with sudden tears.

"All right, and if I did?" she answered swiftly. "At least I've never admitted as much to Kate. She may suspect a mild affair and have the normal feminine reaction, but she has no reason to suppose I would take Robert from her — just the opposite. Kate is quite safe from losing Robert if she wants him."

He observed her thoughtfully but with a more professional eye, noting that her face was a little thinner and she was making an effort to control her voice.

"You should get away," he said. "Find another job until you're your own mistress and can please yourself."

"How can I? Mr. Brown won't hear of a change and it's no good running away. The allowance has always been paid to whoever was in charge of me and now it comes through Kate. I could hardly expect to find a job which would keep and house me as I am trained for nothing that's marketable."

"Yes, I see. A strange man, your benefactor — possibly

a mild pathological case, if one but knew. What reason did you give for wishing to leave?"

"Oh, just that the place didn't suit me. Kate wouldn't sack me, so I had to be a bit vague."

"It didn't occur to you to give the real reason?"

"The real reason?"

"Emotional disturbance — even, being the object of unwelcome attentions. I would have thought in the light of this gentleman's apparent views on unsuitable admirers it would have been your strongest card." There was a definite twinkle in his eye as he spoke and she gave him that slow, engaging smile.

"Yes, it would, wouldn't it?" she said. "And I could come clean with impunity as Mr. Brown is a stranger and doesn't know any of us. I could confess without naming any names that I'd had the misfortune to fall for a man whose intentions were none too clear and would he please see fit to remove me from temptation."

"Very masterly! I can see your imagination will never let you down in a crisis," he said with some dryness, and her eyes immediately became grave.

"It isn't all imagination," she told him frankly. "I have a horrid feeling that if the week-end hadn't ended as it did, I might have been persuaded to whatever course Robert had in mind for the future. Now you know what I wouldn't confess to another living soul, John, but doctors are safe, like priests and lawyers, aren't they?"

"Yes, my dear, and I'm honoured by your confidence," he said a shade formally, and wondered for the first time if he had misjudged Robert Farmer. For all his dislike, he did not think he was the type of man who would seduce a young girl in his cousin's employ. It was more likely that he realised the child was becoming fonder of him than he wished and for that very reason was keeping away.

"Thank you," she said, and reached up a hand to him. "Dear John . . . I do hope things turn out well for you. Even if Kate is still fond of Robert in that way, she's very practical when it comes to deciding what's best for Timmy, and a doctor would be far more satisfactory as a father than an up-and-coming barrister with his nose forever stuck in his briefs from morning to night."

At this he burst out laughing and got into his car.

"Well, I don't know that that's a very encouraging comparison, but I'll take it in the spirit in which it was meant. Look after yourself, Victoria, and remember the world is seldom well lost for love," he said, turning on the ignition.

"Kate said the same thing to me once, so you must think alike on certain matters, mustn't you?" she replied, sounding suddenly quite gay, and he made a wry face out of the window and drove away without comment.

July brought a return of more settled weather and Victoria, when Timmy did not need her, found compensation for the rejection of her plans by working in the garden, weeding and trying to catch up on the vigorous signs of Sam's neglect. But if the warm summer days restored her to an acceptance of her situation, they did little to soothe Elspeth's temper and she remarked rather acidly after some trivial domestic argument one morning that it was high time Mr. Rab paid them a visit and put an end to moods and contrariness, for, said she, it was plain as the nose on your face that the house hadn't been the same since he was last down and if Mrs. Allen was too stiff-necked to invite him then Victoria should do it instead.

"Oh, no, it's not my place," Victoria answered primly, but received a withering look in exchange.

"Hoots! Do you think I don't ken what goes on in this house, under my verra nose?" she retorted, her native burr becoming very apparent. "Since you saw fit to quarrel with the gentleman and send him from the house without his supper it's for you to swallow your pride and call him back. You can tell Mr. Rab that Mrs. Allen is missing him and it's time Timmy had that present he was promised a long time since."

Victoria obediently wrote to Robert, adopting Elspeth's suggestions and rather overdoing Kate's need of his company. She also wrote to Mr. Brown reiterating her desire to leave Farthings and remembering the doctor's advice, set down a candid analysis of the regrettable state of her heart. It was not, she thought upon re-reading this effusion, a very lucid explanation of the situation, since Robert must necessarily remain anonymous and it was difficult to bare one's soul to a perfect stranger who, for all she knew, might not even trouble to read the letter.

It was Kate who heard first, and as she passed the letter to Victoria across the breakfast table it seemed plain from her expresion that she was both hurt and displeased.

"I thought we had agreed to forget this business and carry on as before," she said. "Why have you stirred up fresh trouble?"

Victoria made no reply until she had digested the ambiguous contents of Mr. Chapple's careful communication, then she said quietly:

"I suppose they wanted to be sure I wasn't just romancing. There's no suggestion of blame where you're concerned, Kate. They only want assuring that you consider the situation warrants the inconvenience of making other arrangements."

"And were you romancing? Since, with typical legal caution, they are careful to avoid direct accusations, it's not very clear what the situation amounts to. Had you implied that you were being subjected to unwelcome attentions?"

"No—no, of course not! I—I simply tried to explain my real reasons for wanting to leave without involving anyone."

"Which are?"

"But you know, Kate. It clearly cut no ice to say the place didn't suit me, so I thought I'd better come clean."

"And lay the blame at Robert's door, I suppose, by way of clinching the matter. Why in that case, have you written asking him to come down?"

"Have you heard from Robert, then?" Victoria asked.

"He rang up last night about another matter and mentioned it in passing."

"Oh!"

"Your invitation hardly accords very well with the tale you seem to have spun for Mr. Brown's benefit, does it?"

"Oh, Kate, can't you *see?*" Victoria exclaimed, wishing she had never paid attention to either John Squires' or Elspeth's counsel. "I only tried to convince him that I'd got myself into an emotional tangle, and I wrote to Robert

136

because I thought he might be stopping away on account of that and it wasn't fair to you."

"Somewhat muddled reasoning, but I suppose I must accept it. Are you sure you're not trying to deceive yourself because you're still smarting from that unfortunate affair of the roses?"

"Perhaps it wasn't so unfortunate as it appeared at the time. Unkind practical jokes have a very salutary effect on emotional misconceptions," Victoria replied with gentle evasion, and Kate sighed.

"Yes," she said, "I can understand that. Still, you've had time to reconsider, and though I hold no brief for silly pranks there must have been some good reason to trigger off that one."

"Such as?"

Kate hesitated.

"Well," she replied a little lamely, "he probably thought roses from Mr. Brown would crown the birthday for you, as indeed it did, and if I hadn't unwittingly caught him out and you hadn't eavesdropped, you would have gone on living quite happily in your fool's paradise, wouldn't you?"

"Yes, and that should answer you, Kate. No one but a complete moron is satisfied to go about in blinkers," Victoria retorted, and Kate, regretting too late her choice of words, folded the lawyer's letter back into its meticulous creases and sat tapping it irritably against her thumbnail.

"Yes, of course. Well, what do you want me to answer to this?" she said, and her voice was cool and brisk again.

"You could say," Victoria suggested gravely, "that young girls are sometimes apt to mistake idle attentions for something deeper and you think, in the circumstances, a change would be advisable."

"And did you?"

"If I did it's all in the past, but it's a good enough reason for the lawyers. They can hardly refuse to regard the matter seriously if you back me up."

"Very well. I wish, though, you could bring yourself to confide in me. Robert has a right to know where he slipped up, quite apart from those wretched roses."

"If he slipped up at all it was in thinking a proposal of

marriage would cancel out other bad jokes," Victoria answered, and Kate smiled, her resentment ebbing a little.

"Poor Victoria," she said softly, "I suspect that you care rather more than you'll admit."

"I don't care at all, and if I did I'm not so far gone that I couldn't get over it."

"In that case you'll have no objection if Robert comes down again soon?"

"Of course not. Would I have written to suggest it if I did?"

"I don't know. I gather you took great pains to put the onus on me."

"Well, you've missed him, haven't you? He may or may not have stopped away on my account, but, as Elspeth pointed out, it's not right that the mistress of the house should be deprived of visitors to suit the whims of a paid employee."

"Dear me!" said Kate quite mildly. "You do seem to have got yourself in a tangle! Who else has been proffering well-meaning advice?"

"Only people who have your well-being at heart."

"I suppose you mean John. And what was his reason for wanting to get you out of the house? Has he, by any chance, fallen a victim to more youthful charms and distrusts Robert's evil influence?" Kate spoke with such sudden bitterness that for a moment Victoria could only sit and blink at her.

"*Kate!*" she exclaimed then, her own anger flaring up, "you know very well John's only got eyes for you. He's the sort of quixotic fool who'd hand you over to someone else without a struggle if he thought it would make you happier. He probably only wants me out of the way to ease the situation for you."

"I'm sorry, I shouldn't have said that," Kate said a little stiffly. "All the same, I think you've probably been more honest with John than you have with me."

"And that was possible because he's only concerned indirectly with my affairs. You should know better than to be jealous on that score, and if you want the truth, I think you treat him abominably! You use him so long as it suits you and trade on his dog-like devotion."

138

"Victoria—be careful!" warned Kate, going a little white. "I've allowed you the freedom of a friend and an equal since you've been here, but I won't put up with impertinence. I'll go and reply to that letter now and you can take it to the post when it's ready. I shall have no difficulty this time in persuading the lawyers that a change is not only advisable but necessary — both from your employer's point of view and your own. If they are still unwilling to make other arrangements for the little time that's left, then I must demand an audience with the reluctant Mr. Brown in person — a demand you could well have insisted on yourself in the circumstances had you not been more content to dwell in your cloud-cuckoo-land." She got up as she finished speaking, the letter in her hand, and left the room, closing the door behind her with a sharp click of finality.

A gust of wind caught the curtains at the open casement windows and sent them spiralling out into the room while in the distance the first faint growl of thunder echoed over the downs, and Victoria, still sitting stiffly in her place at the breakfast table, suddenly bowed her face in her hands. She wept not only for the unthinking dissolution of a friendship, but for the lost felicity of her foolish dreams.

CHAPTER NINE

IT was to be a week of thundery weather with storms that threatened but never came to much, leaving the atmosphere sticky and oppressive. The heavy showers which punctuated the sultry closeness pressing down on the countryside were never long enough to relieve the thirsty earth and only beat down the tall flowers in Kate's herbaceous border which Victoria had tied up and staked with such care only a week ago.

"I wish," she observed after days of exhausting heat, "we could have one good, cracking storm and have done with it."

"That, perhaps, is being held in reserve," Kate answered ambiguously, using the polite, measured tones she had employed since their disastrous altercation, and Victoria's enquiring glance held a modicum of wariness.

"Was that a metaphorical observation?" she asked, trying to match Kate's casual coolness.

"You can take it how you like," Kate replied, raising her eyebrows. "Perhaps I was simply anticipating a final clearing of the air."

Victoria, taking the remark literally, asked quickly:

"Have you heard from the solicitors, then?"

"Not yet, but I've heard from Robert. He'll be down this week-end."

"Oh!"

"Perhaps," observed Kate, catching a suggestion of dismay in the exclamation, "you've had time to regret your hasty intervention on my behalf. It's a pity your excellent Miss Scott lives so far away in Wales or you might have begged a bed for the week-end."

"I'm not," replied Victoria, stung to retaliation, "in the least anxious to avoid a meeting with Robert, but if I'm going to be in the way I can quite well make myself scarce."

"What nonsense! If you're going to be tiresomely tactful without any encouragement you'll simply embarrass us both. Now, run along and get Timmy up from his rest.

140

After tea we'll play Happy Families and allow him to cheat a little because he's being extra good."

As the week drew to a close, Victoria found herself looking forward to Robert's visit with a mixture of anticipation and dread. Whatever his intentions might once have been he was, she knew, much too experienced and worldly-wise to allow awkwardness to spoil his week-end, neither was he likely to commit the folly of arriving with floral tributes as a peace-offering. She wondered whether he would allude at all to his last visit or whether absence and time for more sober reflection had turned his thoughts back to Kate. It was, she realised with a sudden sharp awareness, very likely the last time she would see him, for soon Mr. Brown must make his intentions known. When next he came she would be gone and life at Farthings would go on without her. For one panic-stricken moment she wished with all her heart that she could have been gone before the ordeal of another meeting, but by constantly reminding herself how successfully he had made a fool of her, she was able to whip up a comforting illusion of indifference.

Robert was expected in time for dinner on Friday and all day the house had exuded an air of occasion. Elspeth, miraculously restored to good humour, was clearly determined to show her approval by excelling herself in culinary skill, and set Victoria to work washing the best china and polishing silver between numerous errands to the village for forgotten delicacies. Timmy, finding himself neglected in consequence, caused a minor panic by taking himself off unaccompanied down the hill, to be brought back by John Squires, who had chanced to spot him making a determined assault on a neighbour's strawberry beds. The doctor was not unwilling, Victoria thought, to find a legitimate excuse for calling after his last unhappy visit and Kate could do no less than offer him a glass of sherry together with demure surprise at his absence. She seemed a little piqued when he observed that Victoria was looking washed out and airily blamed the weather, adding innocently that Elspeth was killing the fatted calf in honour of Robert's arrival and poor Victoria was being run off her feet with last-minute preparations.

"Oh, I see. And is it an occasion of any special significance? I thought, since he's practically part of the family, he's used to just taking pot luck," John said casually, but his eyes still rested thoughtfully on Victoria's averted face and Kate gave a small, indecisive shrug.

"Yes, well . . . he hasn't been down for some time and you know what Elspeth is. Nothing's too good for Mr. Rab and we're all of us a bit in need of cheering up," she replied, and his eyebrows lifted.

"Really? This young woman looks more in need of a tonic than a gay week-end. Come to my surgery next time you're in the village, Victoria, and I'll give you a prescription," he said.

"I've no doubt she'll pick up once she's away from here," Kate observed before Victoria could reply, and he smiled, but his eyes were a little rueful as he said to Victoria:

"So you took my advice, and it's done the trick?"

"I don't know. We're still waiting to hear," Victoria replied, not caring very much for the trend the conversation was taking, and Kate said as she observed the doctor's quick frown:

"Don't you think you were rather rash to meddle John? Whatever Victoria may have told you, she was settled enough here until her head was turned by a couple of well-intentioned admirers." She spoke quite pleasantly, even with a touch of amused indulgence, but Victoria sprang to her feet, the colour standing out sharply on her cheekbones.

"If you'll excuse me, Kate, I'll go and get Timmy cleaned up for lunch. I don't think John would be very interested in my hypothetical admirers," she said.

"Was that quite fair?" the doctor asked when the sound of her hurried flight up the corner staircase had died away, and Kate lowered her eyes.

"No, it wasn't," she said, and got up to refill both their glasses, spilling a few drops of sherry because her hand was not quite steady. "I don't know what's the matter with me, John, unless this oppressive heat is getting us all down. Perhaps it's I and not Victoria who's in need of medical advice."

"Would you take it, Kate?"

"It would depend on the remedy, wouldn't it?"

"Perhaps the remedy is simpler and pleasanter than you think."

She sat down again, sipping her sherry rather quickly, and regarded him with troubled enquiry, but the old warmth was back in her eyes.

"I—I've been unfair to you, John," she said then. "Victoria took me to task and we quarrelled over you, since then we don't seem able to get back on the old footing, but she was right. Is it possible to be jealous but heartwhole at the same time, do you suppose?"

"One can feel possessive about a person without wishing to be possessed in return, I imagine, which might result in a sort of dog-in-the-manger form of jealousy," he replied with some dryness, and she made a wry face at him.

"Not a very attractive picture," she said. "I've always prided myself on being free of the more obvious weaknesses of my sex, but it seems I am wrong."

"Dear Kate, don't scorn your very natural imperfections — they make you so much more approachable," he said, and she looked at him with startled eyes.

"Approachable? But I'm the least self-satisfied of people!" she exclaimed, sounding quite hurt.

"Very true, but that's not quite what I meant. I was only implying that I find a touch of feminine inconsistency in you encouraging. Long associations, however unsentimental, have deep roots. Would you have married Farmer?"

She finished the last of her sherry and placed the empty glass on a table beside her with careful deliberation.

"Perhaps," she said, sounding a little regretful. "It was such a pleasant, undemanding relationship . . . we made a family without the ties of necessity and — and it was so good for Timmy to have a man about the place. I just drifted."

"And now?"

She sighed, looking a little rueful. "And now there's Victoria, and I've no means of gauging how deep that's gone. Robert played a silly trick which had unfortunate results and perhaps it jolted her out of a mood that was merely infatuation, in which case, it was just as well. The young have tender feelings, but not a great sense of pro-

143

portion. It takes time to get one's emotional sights into focus."

"Not necessarily. That young woman, thanks to her unusual circumstances, has acquired quite a philosophy. Does Farmer know she's leaving you?"

"Not unless she told him when she wrote, and I don't imagine she did."

"H'm . . . interesting to observe the reaction."

"It will be more than interesting if he suspects his name has been introduced for the purpose of softening up Mr. Brown," Kate retorted with a brisk return to tartness, and John got to his feet saying it was time he was off.

"Don't *you* lose your sense of proportion, my dear," he said with a twinkle. "It isn't likely Victoria would have given anything away other than her own feelings. She's hardly on confidential terms with her Invisible Man."

"No, I suppose not, I'm beginning to suspect he's really at the root of half the trouble," Kate snapped back impatiently. "If he'd declared himself in the first place and given the poor child some sort of anchorage for her starved affections, she wouldn't have fallen for the first man to take a flattering interest in her. Mr. Brown, whoever he may be, has a lot to answer for in my opinion, and it would give me great pleasure to tell him so to his face."

"A sentiment I heartily endorse," he replied with a grin. "It seems unlikely either of us will get the chance, however, since I have a shrewd suspicion that he intends to remain a mystery to the end. Good-bye for now, dear, troubled Kate, and whatever this weekend may bring, let things take their course. You know where to find me if I'm wanted."

As evening approached Victoria found herself listening for the sound of a car drawing up at the gates which would give her time to make herself scarce and allow Kate to offer a welcome in private, but after all, she was caught unprepared. She had run downstairs in her slip to retrieve the dress she had been ironing in the kitchen and forgotten at the very moment Robert walked into the house.

"No need to be bashful on my account. It isn't the first time I've been greeted by a lady in her underwear," he observed as she turned to run back upstairs, and at the remembered little flick of mockery in his voice she sat down rather abruptly on the bottom tread.

"I'm not the bashful type," she managed to retort with a comforting flash of the old spirit, "and I can well believe that you're fully acquainted with the details of feminine underwear!"

"I'm glad to see you haven't lost your gift for repartee, I'd feared I might be treated with cool disdain which would have been very dull," he said, and advancing further into the hall, laid a florist's beribboned creation on the brassbound chest.

Victoria stared at the flowers in growing indignation and exclaimed: "Oh *no!*" then became aware of his brows raised in quizzical amusement while he stood looking down at her with eyes that were suddenly a little cool.

"Don't jump to unwarrantable conclusions," he said with a very slight drawl. "The flowers are for Kate, on whose behalf you thoughtfully drew my attention to too long an absence."

"Oh, I see. Well, if you'll excuse me, I'll find my frock and go and finish dressing."

"Find your frock? Are you in the habit of mislaying your garments, or am I to assume I've arrived at an inopportune moment and there's a follower lurking somewhere in hiding?"

"I wish I could truthfully say there was," she flung back at him, trying to struggle to her feet but finding herself slipping on the polished boards.

"Dear me! And what would Mr. Brown say to that?" he countered, then reached down a helping hand. "Allow me to assist you before that very brief trifle you're wearing rises any higher for decency or the good of my blood pressure."

He lifted her up, paying no attention to protests or resistance, but he did not at once let her go and held her lightly but firmly between his hands while his eyes searched her upturned face with a disconcerting hint of tenderness.

"Dear, belligerent Victoria Mary . . . had you been bracing yourself against this moment?" he asked her softly. "You should know me better than to suppose I would take advantage of past indiscretions. I have my own way of dealing with awkward situations, so don't hold my manner against me."

The hostility which he had aroused in her so deliberately to see her through that moment he had spoken of melted away, leaving her weak and once more vulnerable. If the past indiscretions he had mentioned were intended to refer to a mistaken infatuation on her part or a perverted sense of humour on his she had no means of guessing, but she knew now with depressing certainty that whatever the future held for her, she must go on loving him. Perhaps, she thought with a flash of saving humour, he would one day become just another image on which to feed her imagination, like Mr. Brown. Perhaps she had, from lack of masculine knowledge, already invented a personality for him which did not in fact exist.

"What are you thinking to cause those wrinkles of perplexity?" he asked, and she slipped neatly out of his grasp.

"Nothing of any consequence," she replied, recovering her composure. "Please go into the parlour and wait for Kate and allow me to finish dressing. Elspeth won't be pleased if I keep her very special dinner waiting."

"Oh! Is it a celebration?" he enquired innocently, but there was a look in his eye which boded no good and she stepped aside with relief as Kate came hurrying down the stairs, exclaiming:

"Of course it's a celebration! You've neglected us for too long, Rob, and we've become browned off with each other's company. Have you forgotten to put on a dress in your haste to be first with a welcome, Victoria, or am I just out of step with the latest fashion?"

Victoria smiled mechanically without replying and escaped to the kitchen, but as the door closed behind her she heard Robert say still with that note of mockery:

"Do I detect a slight flavour of pussiness, dear cousin, or do I merely flatter my masculine ego?"

Kate made some laughing reply which Victoria did not

catch and their voices died away as they went into the parlour and shut the door.

Upstairs in her room Victoria lingered over the finishing touches to her appearance in order to give Kate time for whatever she might have to say to Robert in private, but it soon became clear that Timmy's demands had taken priority and a visit to the nursery was now in progress, judging by the squeals and laughter drifting down the passage which would leave little margin for confidences before Elspeth sounded the gong for dinner. It was as good a way as any of bridging the gap, Victoria thought as she joined the nursery party, but Timmy, sitting up in bed amidst a litter of string and paper wrappings, gave his mother no time for the tactful explanations she had doubtless reserved for a more propitious moment.

"*You* won't let my Toria go away, will you, Uncle Rob?" he demanded.

"Is she going away?" Robert said after a brief pause, and his eyes rested for a moment on Victoria standing uncertainly in the doorway.

"She won't if you say she's not to. It's that Brown person making spells again. He's really a wizard, you know."

"Don't be silly, Timmy, he's nothing of the sort," Kate said rather sharply. "And if Victoria wants to leave us, Uncle Rob can't stop her."

"*Can't* you, Uncle Rob? But I heard you say—" the boy began bouncing up and down with excitement, but Robert interrupted, at the same time pressing him firmly back on to his pillow:

"Never mind what you thought you heard me say, young man. One doesn't repeat what isn't intended for one's ears, and it's time you settled down and went to sleep, anyway."

Back again in the parlour, with drinks at their elbows he said to Kate:

"Why didn't you tell me?"

"I've hardly had a chance since you arrived, have I?" she protested with some truth.

"No, but we've spoken on the telephone."

"Only to fix up this week-end. Besides, I imagined if

147

Victoria wanted you to know, she would have told you herself."

"Did you, Kate? Well, it's of little consequence. When does she want to leave?"

"You don't sound very surprised. As usual, we are waiting upon Mr. Brown's pleasure."

"I see. And what if he continues to disregard his protégée's whims?"

"I don't think he will this time, since I've made my own wishes clear."

"I see," he said again. "Have you and Victoria fallen out?"

"In a manner of speaking, but I do honestly believe a change is called for. You're largely to blame Robert. If you were really serious when you told me you wanted to marry her you've gone a very odd way about things, and I don't imagine that's the impression she has given Mr. Brown."

"Oh? Do I take it then that I'm the villain of the piece?"

"I've no idea, I'm not in Victoria's confidence. You'd better ask John," Kate said rather shortly, and his eyebrows rose.

"Dear me! Am I to assume that the faithful doctor is in danger of transferring his affections?"

"I wouldn't know," she replied with an unconvincing air of indifference, "but she certainly took his advice in the matter of providing Mr. Brown with a more substantial reason for leaving. Whether he, or the lawyers, take a serious view of the situation is yet to be known, but I for one think it's time that gentleman took his responsibilities more actively. It wouldn't hurt him to pay us a casual visit without letting on who he is."

"Very true, but for all you know he may have done just that. Now I come to think of it I wonder it's never occurred to Victoria's lively imagination. You could both of you have gained much entertainment by inventing hidden identities for casual callers, or the vicar — or even the doctor with his fatherly interest and good advice. Now there is a man who might well feel impelled towards philanthropy without letting his noble intentions be known,"

148

Robert said with rather disconcerting enjoyment, and she smiled, though without much amusement.

"Very likely," she retorted, "but John, though he's comfortably off and has a good practice, can hardly be described as a rich tycoon, and Mr. Brown's little whim must have cost him plenty."

"No more than the keep and education of the daughter of any well-to-do parents, and you've no valid reason for inventing rich tycoons," he said, getting to his feet as Victoria came into the room.

"We were discussing the probable or improbable identity of your patron, Victoria. Has it occurred to you that the attentive Dr. Squires might well fill the bill?" he continued, pouring her a glass of sherry.

"For heaven's sake! Don't go putting fresh nonsense into the poor child's head!" Kate exclaimed, observing the gleam of interest which momentarily brightened the girl's eyes, but Victoria was used by now to Robert's methods of getting a rise and became aware at the same time that Kate was not enjoying this latest flight of fancy.

"That of course would be a very happy ending if it were in any way likely, but even my fertile imagination hasn't grasped at that straw," she said, and caught Robert's faint smile of appreciation as he handed her the sherry.

"I don't know that the worthy doctor would care to be likened to a straw, but we'll let that pass," he said, observing with interest the indignant glint in Kate's brown eyes, and Victoria, also noticing, gave him a chilly glance.

"John Squires is good and kind and worth ten of you," she said, and his eyes held a fleeting twinkle.

"I bow to your superior knowledge," he replied with mock humility. "And now let's settle for a pleasant weekend and a return to less controversial matters."

Once seated round the table, Robert steered the conversation into mundane channels with considerable skill, and insisted on Elspeth being summoned to the dining-room to have her health drunk.

"Och, get away with you, Mr. Rab! Have you no better excuse for a toast than a plain body that's paid to cook your vittles?" she retorted with uncompromising bluntness, and her eyes dwelt for a moment on Kate but lingered longest on Victoria, who sat, her face pale and politely attentive in the candlelight while she remembered the almost identical details of that last special occasion. As if he had guessed her thoughts, Robert said softly:

"Only the champagne is missing. I should have thought of that, shouldn't I, Elspeth?"

"Aye, you should, but one wine is as good as another for the purpose. Have you no other tricks up your sleeve, Mr. Rab?" Elspeth said. "It may be the last chance you'll have for wishing Miss Toria well."

"Thanks for the reminder," he replied casually, "but since I understand Miss Toria's departure still requires the sanction of authority, I will give you Mr. Brown — may his schemes prosper and his shadow never grow less!" He solemnly raised his glass and drank, and almost without volition, Kate and Victoria followed suit, but Elspeth set her glass down on the table unfinished and made for the door.

"And that's a toast I'll no' be troubling with! Shame on you, Mr. Rab, for making fun of an occasion that should be serious! Mr. Brown, indeed! If any such pairson exists, he's no better than a bogle to frighten the bairns with!" she exclaimed, her accent broadening in outrage, and she stalked out of the room.

For a moment there was an astonished silence, then Kate and Victoria succumbed simultaneously to giggles.

"Oh!" gasped Kate, wiping her eyes. "*Poor* Mr. Brown — just a bogle to frighten the bairns with!"

"Many a true word spoken in jest," observed Robert, whose laughter had been rather more perfunctory. "Haven't you been obedient to orders for rather too long, Victoria Mary?" He did not speak with any great seriousness, but her merriment was quenched.

"I've had no choice," she replied gravely. "Besides, debts have to be paid in whatever coin is stipulated and, bogle or not, I have nothing but gratitude for Mr. Brown."

"And to what extreme might that carry you?" he asked, his manner suddenly as sober as hers, and Kate, conscious that she was momentarily redundant, murmured some excuse and left the room.

"Well?" said Robert, absently snuffing out a guttering candle between finger and thumb.

"I don't know," she said nervously, scooping up breadcrumbs into neat little piles beside her plate. "It would depend on what was asked, but as the only demands have been purely functional all these years, I'm not likely to be put to the test, am I?"

"Oh, you never know! Even the most amiable of Shylocks has a habit of exacting his pound of flesh," he replied with a lightness that was far from reassuring, and she looked across at him with widening eyes.

"Do you mean he might be a money-lender? I never thought of that," she said, and he pushed back his chair with an irritable little jerk.

"No, I don't," he replied, beginning to snuff out the remaining candles. "I was speaking figuratively, as you are quite intelligent enough to know. Now, we'd better abandon this unrewarding topic and go and join Kate who, with the best of intentions, has made a tactful, if unnecessary withdrawal," he said, and blew out the last of the candles.

The curtains had been left undrawn across the windows since the evening was very sultry and something of daylight still remained, but with the dousing of the candles the room seemed suddenly dark and Victoria, groping her way to the door, stumbled against Robert. He put out a hand to steady her, holding her against him for a moment, and she said a little breathlessly:

"What are you after, Robert? Why are you treating everything as if it didn't matter?"

"Don't you know?"

"Not really — unless you're trying to let me down lightly. I wasn't planning to treat you to — to sentimental recriminations when I asked you to come down."

"Weren't you? What a pity. Still, there's no reason why you should suppose I feared recriminations, was there? After all, it was you who turned *me* down."

"Yes . . . yes, I did, didn't I?" she said, sounding rather surprised, then confused memories of the insulting implication of that untimely proposal stiffened her weakening resolve.

"You could hardly," she said, trying to wriggle out of

his suddenly tightened grip, "have expected me to fall into your arms with gratitude at a rather obvious attempt to soothe my feelings."

"I'm not the type to deal in soothing syrup, as you should know by now," he retorted, his voice a little rough above her head, "but you chose to be bloody-minded in order to save your silly little pride and you've only yourself to blame if the whole thing's backfired on you."

"What do you mean, backfired? Are you flattering yourself that I have regrets?"

"Well, haven't you? I should hate to think that all this sound and fury has no more reality than the one-sided imaginary scenes you probably indulge in with the absent Mr. Brown."

"How dare you mock at my dreams? How dare you mock at Mr. Brown who, if nothing else, has cared enough to give me the start in life my father had planned for me?" she burst out, and heard him sigh as he gently released her.

"Dear, stubborn little ostrich — I would never mock at your dreams, but they're sometimes more pertinent than you think. As for Mr. Brown, I'm of the opinion that it's high time that gentleman revealed himself or left the field to less exalted persons. I, for one, am beginning to find him a bore."

As she lay tossing in bed that night, unable to sleep for the heat, and the conflicting emotions which troubled her spirit, Victoria bitterly regretted her impulse to make peace with Robert for Kate's sake. It was years since she had consoled herself with imaginary meetings with Mr. Brown and still more unlikely happy endings, but the subterfuge still worked. Her limbs relaxed and her eyelids grew heavy as she conjured up pictures of a faceless old gentleman who listened gravely to her grievances and patted her kindly on the head. "There, there, my dear, it's all for the best. I never did like that browbeating barrister, so just forget him," he was saying comfortingly as she fell asleep, and he must have continued talking right through her dreams, for when she woke a voice was saying: "Forget your dreams, my dear. I've brought you a surprise."

Victoria opened her eyes, still hazy with sleep, but it was

152

only Kate standing by her bed with a breakfast tray, a quizzical smile twisting her lips.

"You were smiling most charmingly in your sleep," she said. "What were you dreaming about?"

"Mr. Brown. I thought you were him," Victoria answered, still only half awake, and Kate's eyebrows rose.

"Very curious," she observed a shade cynically. "Well, I hope the contents of your letter will match the promise of your dream."

"What letter?"

"The long-awaited answer to yours, one must assume. That's the surprise."

"Oh!" Victoria struggled into a sitting position, snatching at the legal-looking communication, then held it rather gingerly as if she were afraid it might burn her.

"Aren't you going to open it?" Kate asked curiously, but Victoria slipped the letter under her pillow.

"Later," she said briefly, and Kate smiled somewhat doubtfully and sat down on the side of the bed.

"Victoria—" she began a little diffidently, "I don't know whether this will be good or bad news, but whatever it is, try to be philosophical."

"Haven't you heard, too?"

"No, but I didn't put my own views very strongly, despite our unedifying little bout of mud-slinging. I'm very fond of you, my dear, and only want what's best for you. Remember that, won't you?"

Quick tears brightened Victoria's eyes for a moment and she thrust out a willing hand.

"Oh, Kate," she said, "I've been so wretched thinking I must seem so ungrateful, after all you've done for me."

"I've done nothing but employ you, so don't go making mountains out of molehills. If it so happened that I also felt affection for you, there's no need to feel beholden for that," Kate answered with her more familiar briskness, and Victoria gave her that slow, lifting smile which had been noticeably absent these past days.

"Dear Kate . . ." she said with lingering fondness, "I'm so glad to think you may miss me a little when I'm gone."

"Don't rush your fences! You won't know till you open that letter what the immediate future may hold. That's why

153

I counselled philosophy. Do you really want to go, Victoria? Hasn't Robert talked any sense into you?"

"If you mean did he use persuasion when you so tactfully left us alone after dinner, no, he didn't. He was much too occupied sharpening his wits and his tongue at my expense to indulge in any helpful conversation," Victoria replied coolly and seemingly without concern, and Kate said:

"Oh, dear, I had rather hoped . . . still, you should know Robert by this time. He has curious ways of bringing about his intentions," she said.

"His intentions, I think, were never very clear or very serious, dear Kate, so don't distress yourself on that count. Now, if you'll agree, I'd like to take Timmy for a picnic if the weather holds. That will give *you* time to have sense talked in to you."

As soon as the door had closed behind her, Victoria pushed her plate away and snatched the letter from under her pillow. She did not know why she had felt such a strong desire to read it in private, but now that she was alone she could restrain her curiosity no longer.

Mr. Brown had been disturbed by the news conveyed to him in her letter of the 5th inst., Mr. Chapple had written. He considered it unwise, however, to seek fresh employment for so short a period, since his plans for the future had been cut and dried for some time. He was prepared to arrange a meeting at once in order to put certain propositions before her. Mr. Brown, Mr. Chapple pointed out with rather coy ambiguity, was neither senile nor in poor health, so he trusted that in view of past advantages she would look favourably upon his suggestions. If she would call at their city branch on Monday next, the 15th, at eleven-thirty precisely, Mr. Brown would make himself known to her and put forward his plans for their mutual consideration. They were, hers faithfully, etc. . . .

"*Well,* blow me down!" she exclaimed inelegantly, and sprang out of bed. She couldn't wait to get dressed before imparting such momentous news to Kate and without troubling with dressing-gown or slippers, raced downstairs in her pyjamas.

But Kate was nowhere about and it was Robert who appeared in answer to her excited shouts, the morning paper tucked under his arm.

"Dear me, what slovenly habits for this hour of day," he observed, eyeing her state of undress with interest. "Is the house on fire?"

"Of course not, but I want to find Kate. I've had the most extraordinary letter from Mr. Chapple," she replied. "You wouldn't *believe*, Robert, what seems to have been simmering in that man's mind!"

"What, old Chapple?"

"No, of course not — Mr. *Brown!* I'm to meet him on Monday at half-past eleven to discuss certain propositions."

"H'm . . . sounds fishy to me. He's probably a dirty old man. May I see the letter?"

"No, you may not — not before Kate's read it, anyway. You'll only make fun of it. Where is she?"

"At the bottom of the garden, I believe, pulling lettuces for your lunch."

She found Kate in the vegetable garden, inspecting the lettuces with a dissatisfied eye and bemoaning the fact that most of them had been eaten by slugs.

"I don't know why I keep that boy on," she complained. "He's never here when he's wanted and when he is he skimps his work."

"Never mind the slugs — read this!" Victoria said, thrusting Mr. Chapple's letter into her hands. "I always told you I would meet Mr. Brown one day, and now it's coming true."

"H'm . . ." Kate murmured, much as Robert had done when she had reached the end. "Several conclusions could be drawn from this. Well, Victoria, are you going? He doesn't give you much time, I must say."

"But of course! Haven't I been waiting for this moment ever since it all began?"

"Yes, I suppose so. I didn't really think it would happen, you know. I've never quite been able to swallow Mr. Brown."

"Because you thought he was just a figurehead — something to represent a trust and nothing more."

"Yes, I expect I did. Victoria, do you think you're wise? You've made so many images, so many happy-ever-after endings . . . sometimes it's best to keep one's dreams intact." Kate sounded uneasy and her eyes were grave, but

155

Victoria, although a little damped by this guarded reception, was too excited to let doubts disturb her.

"Dear Kate, this *is* the happy ending," she said. "Whoever he may be, Mr. Brown has kept and educated me and now it seems he has planned for me too. The least I can do is to listen to his proposals and fall in with them if I can."

"Listen, yes, but think twice before agreeing. However much you may have benefited by his generosity, he doesn't own you," Kate said a little dryly. "Has Robert seen this letter?"

"No. Anyway, it's nothing to do with him."

"He mightn't agree with that. Anyway, I think we'll let him read it. His advice on legal matters is to be respected."

But Robert had no advice to offer. Indeed he adopted a somewhat frivolous attitude when later, Victoria, bathed and dressed, joined the cousins on the patio for mid-morning coffee. He insisted on reading the letter aloud, interspersed with conjectures and speculations as wild and unlikely as any Victoria might have thought up, until she was reduced to giggles and Kate to exasperation.

"But seriously, Rob, don't you think she should insist on more definite details concerning these vague propositions before committing herself to an interview that might prove embarrassing?" Kate said. "I think she should have more time. It's extremely short notice considering the many opportunities there have been in the past. Ring up and make another date, Victoria."

"Nonsense!" Robert said unhelpfully. "The gentleman might change his mind. Anyway, there won't be anyone in the office on a Saturday. As it happens I have an appointment with old Chapple myself on Monday, so Victoria can drive up with me, which will save her finding her own way."

"Oh, in that case I shall have fewer doubts. You can always insist on meeting the gentleman yourself, can't you?" said Kate, sounding relieved, but Victoria, who did not take at all kindly to this unexpected turn of events, said quickly:

"I think you've just made that up, Robert, What business could you possibly have with Chapple, Chapple & Ponsonby?"

"Business that will, I trust, prove pleasantly lucrative.

You must have forgotten that barristers have to depend on solicitors for their briefs," Robert replied with a touch of amusement, and she coloured.

"Oh! Well, I'd just as soon go up by train."

"And I'd just as soon you didn't. No, no, my child, you must humour me in this. I can assure you I have no intention of cramping your style when we get there, but it's making rather heavy weather, don't you think, to arrive at the same destination by separate routes just to be awkward — besides, it will clearly relieve Kate's mind," he said and she could do no less than give in, albeit with deep misgivings. If her anxiety to oblige Mr. Brown sprang largely from a desire to escape from Robert, it was not going to help her resolution to have him virtually handing her over.

"Well," said Kate briskly, "that's one thing settled to my satisfaction. I shall feel much happier knowing Robert will be holding a watching brief for you, my dear. He may seem to be treating this business rather casually, but he won't let you sign away your freedom. Now, if you want to find a quiet spot for your picnic before trippers get there first, you ought to be starting. Don't stay out too long, will you? It may be working up for a storm."

"Oh, no — not today!" Victoria exclaimed, springing to her feet with alacrity, glad that she could escape from them both and recapture in private the first fine flavour of her small miracle. "There's not a cloud in the sky, and nothing is going to spoil my red-letter day."

"Famous last words," Robert murmured as she ran into the house. "Let's hope Providence is too occupied with higher things to be tempted."

CHAPTER TEN

ALAS for Victoria's confident predictions, the day was
to end in near disaster. She had driven along by-roads and
narrow lanes that were strange to her once the village was
left behind before finding a suitable spot in which to picnic. She was governed by the age-old urge to find something better round the next corner and by the time hunger
had driven them to stop by a stretch of woodland which
promised shade and solitude she had little notion of where
they were.

It was a delightful wood with grassy rides which enticed
them further and further into its unkown depths, and so
isolated from the familiar world did it seem, Victoria would
not have been surprised to come upon the gingerbread
house which had lured Hansel and Gretel to their encoun-
ter with the witch. She felt quite relieved when the ride
opened out suddenly into a cheerful little glade which
boasted a mossy carpet to sit on and sunlight filtering invitingly through the high trees. Even Timmy seemed glad
to abandon exploration for the moment and eat his lunch
in the safety of the less shadowy clearing.

By the time they had finished their lunch it had become
very close and still, but the tracery of leaves and branches
above them allowed glimpses of the sky too small for any
warning signs of a change in the weather. Victoria lay
back on the warm dry moss, stretching her limbs drowsily
and closing her eyes to evoke more clearly the images she
had fashioned for herself throughout the years. After Monday there would be no need to dream, no need to wonder
. . . no need, even, to remember that she had been fooled
into false hopes on account of five dozen roses sent by
another man. This was a train of thought, however, that
led to mental pictures which only proved disturbing, for
Robert's image, she found, became superimposed on that
other, reducing it to wraithlike proportions. She tried not
to think of him, to comfort herself with the knowledge that
Mr. Brown seemed to be offering a way of escape from the
painful stirrings of first love, but it was Robert's face she
remembered last as she fell aleep, his voice following her

into her dreams, saying with that mocking tenderness which meant so little: "Do you find it so difficult to see me in the light of a lover?"

A distant roll of thunder woke her, or perhaps it was the first chill drops of rain stinging her warm bare flesh which startled her into awareness of the coming storm. The wood seemed to have undergone a frightening change while she slept; the little glade was no longer friendly and dappled with sunshine, the rides that led out of it were dark tunnels disappearing into a maw of blackness and, overhead, wind rocked the branches of the high trees in a frenzied dance of menace. Victoria looked round quickly for Timmy, wondering why he had not wakened her. He was nowhere to be seen in the small clearing and she began calling impatiently as she packed away the picnic things. Progress was necessarily slow for a five-year-old with a slight limp and they were undoubtedly in for a soaking before the road and the car would be reached. Her annoyance grew as she got no response; it was no time to be hiding and playing tricks on her, but as the minutes passed and no anwering shout rewarded her, annoyance turned to alarm. She did not know how long she had slept, and if the boy had wandered off to explore the wood on his own, he might well be lost or, even worse, have fallen and hurt himself.

She began running a little way down each ride, calling his name, then thrust her way through the tangle of bushes and undergrowth that ended in the clearing, brambles tearing at her bare legs while whip-like branches snapped back in her face as she tried to part them. It seemed to her hours while she searched and called, running this way and that with panic mounting at every step. It was so dark now in the wood that it was difficult to recognize the outlines of paths and although the rain still held off the thunder grew louder and nearer while lightning streaked through the trees making grotesque shapes of their writhing branches. As she pushed her way back to the edge of the clearing, she stumbled over something which immediately fastened itself round her legs with such terrifying suddenness that she gave a scream.

"Did you think I was a bear?" said Timmy's voice with

a complete absence of distress, and she shook him quite roughly to ease her racing heartbeats.

"Have you been hiding here all the time?" she demanded furiously, and he gave her a complacent affirmative. "Didn't you hear me calling?"

"Yes, but I thought I'd give you a fright."

"Oh, for heaven's sake!" she answered impatiently, then hugged him to her as the storm broke in good earnest directly over their heads. Rain fell with a torrential violence and in a moment they were soaked through; lightning seemed to run down the trunks of trees like fiery snakes and the noise was deafening. Even Timmy lost some of his brashness and clung to her, beginning to whimper, and although she was not normally affected by storms, she experienced a few seconds of atavistic terror. The wood seemed alive with a primaeval fury, threatening to crush them both for their wanton trespass and, as though some unseen force could read her thoughts, there came an answering crack from the heavens, as a ball of fire descended, splitting the trunk of a fir tree from top to bottom. Victoria just had time to thrust the boy back into the bushes before the tree fell with a crash across the clearing, demolishing the picnic basket beneath its weight.

"Was that a thunderbolt?" asked Timmy, awed but still curious.

"I shouldn't think so, but a tree was struck and I think we'd better get out of here," Victoria answered, hoping her voice did not betray her fear.

There were several rides converging on the clearing and for a moment Victoria stood in doubt. The tree which now lay across the open space altered its perspective and in the noise and confusion everything looked different. She thought she remembered that clump of willows on the right as they had come out into the little glade, but halfway down the ride she wasn't so sure. The wood seemed full of willow and the ride more twisting than she remembered, but she pressed on, hoping with every turn to come upon the road. The ground was already waterlogged beneath their feet and every so often they stumbled and fell, trapped by unseen ruts and holes. The boy was beginning to flag and his sense of adventure was already quenched.

"We're nearly there," she assured Timmy as she hastened her steps, but when they rounded the next bend she stopped dead with a little cry of dismay. The path straggled on for a little way, then petered out in a density of trees and bramble which stretched away on all sides as far as the eye could see. The ride had led them back into the very heart of the wood.

"Where's the road?" asked Timmy blankly.

"Where indeed!" she replied with much bitterness.

"You *said* we'd find the road, Toria. Why isn't it here?" he persisted, beginning to whine.

"Because it's somewhere else," she replied with some tartness. "We'll just have to retrace our steps and try another ride — this doesn't lead anywhere."

"It's all your fault — and you said you knew the way," wailed Timmy, beginning to cry, and sat down firmly in the mud.

"Well, I thought I did, but I chose the wrong ride. Now be a brave boy, darling, and stop crying. We'll have a rest before we turn, but we have to go back. You wouldn't like to stay here all night, would you?" She had gone down on her knees in the muddy wetness to coax and comfort the child, feeling badly in need of comfort herself. Would Kate be worrying yet on account of the storm? Had she and Robert settled their affairs during the respite she had given them? Would anything ever be the same again after meeting Mr. Brown on Monday? But Monday seemed a long way off in her present predicament and Mr. Brown as strange and unfriendly as the dark, wet wood which threatened to imprison them . . .

She had no idea how long it took them to retrace their steps, but back again in the clearing, she sat the boy down under the shelter of some bushes while she vainly tried to remember their direction. She had already lost a sandal and she took the other one off and threw it away, too tired by now to care whether her bare feet would carry her any further.

"That's the way . . . a goblin's just made a face at me and run down there . . ." Timmy's voice came to her eerily from under the bushes. He was already half asleep and she pulled him to his feet.

"All right, we'll follow the goblin," she said cheerfully. Short of tossing a coin, it was as good a way as any of deciding which ride to take, but they had not been walking for long before the boy began to cry again.

"My leg's gone funny . . . I think it's broke . . . carry me, Toria," he whimpered.

"Oh, Timmy, I *can't* — you're much too heavy," she protested, wondering if, after all, they would have to spend the night in this horrible wood.

"You can — a piggyback, like Uncle Rob does," he said with a child's complacent disregard for an adult's difficulties.

"Your Uncle Rob is more up to your weight than I am," Victoria countered with some tartness. "All right, I'll try, but don't throttle me."

Progress was, naturally, slowed to a minimum, but she managed somehow. Every so often she trod on a stone which sent a sharp stab of pain through her numbed feet; the boy grew heavier and heavier astride her back and she spared a thought for St. Christopher breasting the torrent with his Burden, but the storm was retreating and although the rain still fell with some violence, the lightning had become intermittent and the thunder no more than a protesting grumble in the distance.

"Timmy, you must try and walk for a bit, now . . . I can't carry you much further," she said at last, too weary to care any longer whether she had chosen the wrong ride again, but Timmy, already refreshed, slid unprotestingly to the ground and ran on ahead, shouting and splashing through the puddles. Presently he came running back to her, crying:

"The road! The road! Only I think perhaps it's just a river."

"More likely a mirage," Victoria commented dryly, following in his wake with little hope that they had come to the end of their journey, but miraculously it was true, and she stood for a moment, staring with unbelieving eyes.

"What's a mirage?" Timmy inevitably demanded, but she hugged him to her half laughing, half crying.

"Something you imagine you see, though you weren't

162

far wrong in mistaking the road for a river," she said, and indeed, the lane which sloped gently down to the next village was awash with a swirling torrent of water spewed out by ditches too blocked or to shallow to hold it.

"Is it a flood, like Noah's Ark?" Timmy asked, sounding suitably impressed, but she bundled him into the waiting car without stopping to embroider on this promising theme and wrapped him up in Kate's old rug which always reposed on the back seat.

"Are you cold?" she asked anxiously, very conscious now that nightmare was behind them, of her responsibility concerning the boy's health, but he shook his head and snuggled down beside her.

"No," he said, proffering a hand. "Feel me. This rug smells of mice."

She felt his hand then tucked it back under the rug, satisfied that he didn't appear to be chilled, aware that she was in less good shape herself and her teeth were beginning to chatter. She pressed the starter button, offering up a silent prayer that the aged Morris would not play one of its favourite tricks and refuse to go, but after a few anxious pushes which produced nothing but ominous whirring noises, the ignition sparked and the car was in motion. It was a brief respite, however. The pedals felt strange and resistant without the support of shoes and Victoria's bare feet kept slipping. She drove too fast down the hill and saw the minor flood at the bottom too late to slow up and take it cautiously. The Morris splashed recklessly through the water, sending up a spray which swamped the radiator, and the engine promptly coughed and died.

"Damn, oh, *damn!* As if we hadn't had enough already!" she exclaimed, and had she been alone, would have eased her frustration in a bout of weeping.

"We need an ark," observed Timmy, peering out at the water with interest, then settled comfortably into sleep.

"Yes, we need an ark," echoed Victoria bitterly. "Failing that, we'll just have to sit here and wait for some passer-by to give us a lift."

They waited for a long time. It was not a road much frequented by traffic and early closing and the storm had kept tradesmen's vans and private cars at home. Eventually it was the driver of a truckload of manure who rescued them, depositing them at the gates of Farthings very late in the afternoon and smelling strongly of dung. Kate, who must have been on the watch, rushed out of the house halfway between relief and anger, followed more leisurely by Robert who stood in the porch surveying the bedraggled pair with some amusement. Timmy, grasping very quickly that he was once more a satisfying centre of attention, gave his mother such a high-coloured account of their adventures that she rounded fiercely on Victoria.

"Hadn't you more sense than to stay in the wood with a storm brewing?" she snapped. "Don't you realise that when that tree was struck it might have fallen on the child?"

"It might have fallen on Victoria, too," Robert murmured from the background, but she ignored the interruption. "And dragging a five-year-old, let alone one that's lame, through mud and brambles because you hadn't the gumption to remember the way! And what about the car?"

"The lorry driver promised he'd stop at the garage on his way to the village. I'm sorry, Kate, none of this was intentional, you know," Victoria said, sounding suddenly rather tearful, and Robert, turning to go back into the house, said over his shoulder:

"Pull yourself together, Kate! Recriminations may relieve your feelings, but they serve no other purpose. Your son, quite clearly, is none the worse for his adventures, so forget your other grievances."

"I'm sorry, Victoria," Kate muttered, turning a little pink. "I only hope, though, that Timmy won't have caught a bad chill. I'll get him into a hot bath at once, and you might ring John in the meantime and ask him to come over."

She hustled the boy into the house and up the stairs, calling to Elspeth to have hot soup ready when the child was in bed, and Victoria remained standing uncertainly in the middle of the hall, aware that her teeth were starting to chatter again.

"You could do with some hot soup yourself, I think Victoria Mary. In the meantime, I would prescribe something stronger," Robert observed, and she became aware that he had propped himself against the oak chest and was regarding her with an amused expression.

"Was Kate very worried?" she asked.

"My charming cousin tends to lose her sense of proportion where her ewe-lamb is involved, as you should know by now," he replied, and she took immediate exception to his apparent air of unconcern.

"Well, at least you were here to boost her morale, or couldn't you be bothered," she snapped, and his eyebrows shot up.

"What an unsympathetic image you still have of me," he observed. "You don't need to be so up in arms. Kate and I understand each other very well."

"Does that mean that you've — settled your affairs?" she asked, and shivered, feeling suddenly very tired and cold.

"I don't know that I quite follow that question, but it's high time you got out of those wet things," he said then, and moving suddenly, took both her hands in his. "You're icy, child, and your teeth sound like castanets. You'd better have the reversion of Timmy's bath in case the hot water doesn't last out. In the meantime go and put on a warm dressing-gown while I fix you a good strong toddy."

The warmth of his hands and the sudden warmth in his eyes were her undoing. His concern for her brought about a swift reaction and she began to weep.

"There, now, my poor child . . . cry it all out . . . there was more in that wood to upset you than a thunderstorm, wasn't there?" he said, and his voice held both tenderness and understanding.

"Yes, there was . . . you were all mixed up with Mr. Brown and I was being m-menaced . . ." she wept.

"Menaced?"

"By the wood . . . I can't explain . . . then Timmy went and hid to pay me out while I was asleep and then we got lost and — and it was all a dreadful nightmare . . . I don't think Timmy is any the worse, though . . . I carried him piggyback the last part of the way . . . my b-back aches . . ."

"I'm not surprised! You're hardly built for such feats of

endurance. Don't take Kate's sharp words too much to heart, my dear — she was frightened, and when one is frightened, one finds relief in hitting out."

She looked up at him with swift enquiry, wondering if he intended the words to mean more than they said, and he smiled down at her and nodded his head.

"Yes," he said, "we all do it at times."

"Even you?"

"Even I. As for you, young woman, you make a positive art of the habit, but don't think you fool me."

"At least I haven't tried to *make* a fool of you, which is altogether different," she retorted, unable to resist an opportunity to renew hostilities in case he should imagine he had sufficiently weakened her defences, but he only grinned and gave her a mild shake.

"Now don't start all that nonsense again, Miss Hayes. One is taught to let bygones be bygones in more charitable circles, so stop bolstering up your ego with false grievances. Go on upstairs, and get those wet thing off."

When she came down again, she found Robert had switched on an electric fire. It was cooler now after the storm and she was glad of the extra warmth for her very bones felt chilled. She sat huddled up in her dressing-gown sipping the whisky Robert brought her and staring at him with puzzled eyes. Every so often she sneezed, and he observed with gentle malice:

"You, my child, are going to have the father and mother of a cold. I doubt you'll be keeping that appointment on Monday."

"Oh, but I must!" she exclaimed, feeling immediately guilty. "The chance may never come again."

"And would that matter?"

"Of course it would matter! Isn't it the one thing I've looked forward to for as long as I can remember?"

"But I fancy the image of Mr. Brown has suffered a sea change of late, or is that wishful thinking on my part?" he murmured gently, and she frowned.

"Why should it be wishful thinking? My feelings for Mr. Brown can hardly matter to you," she retorted, and wished he wasn't so adept at sowing doubts in her mind.

"If that remark was intended to provoke an impassioned denial, I'm afraid you'll be disappointed, Victoria Mary. I have no intention of competing with an imaginary hero," he said with that disconcerting ability to administer a sharp set-down just as matters were looking promising.

"It was no such thing!" she exclaimed indignantly. "I was merely stating an obvious fact. Why should I care if you minded or not?"

"Why, indeed? You've made it very plain that you prefer fiction to fact."

"I don't know what you mean. I may have built up an image for myself for want of anything better, but Mr. Brown is still a fact, however much you don't want to believe in him."

"Yes, yes . . . one can't, I'll agree, accuse poor old Chapple of cooking the whole thing up. I have no doubts concerning your Mr. Brown's existence, only the romantic notions he seems able to inspire in you."

"I've had no romantic notions. If I've thought of him as a father figure it was only natural in the circumstances."

"Ah, but it's been pointed out that he's neither senile nor in poor health, which strikes me as a hint that the suggestions he trusts you will look upon favourably are not necessarily paternal," Robert reminded her with an infuriating air of unconcern, and she took another incautious gulp of whisky which made her choke and cough.

"You really should learn to treat spirits with more respect until you're accustomed to them," he reproved her, adding the final insult to his uncomplimentary innuendoes.

"I'm not a child!" she exclaimed angrily. "In France we had wine with every meal as a matter of course and were taught to recognize a good vintage, too."

"Let us hope, then, you also learnt discretion in other matters."

"If you mean affairs of the heart, there was little opportunity for learning discretion. There never has been much opportunity, now I come to think of it."

She sneezed again and fumbled vainly in the pocket of her dressing-gown for a handkerchief. Robert tossed her his, and the small, intimate gesture accompanied by an indulgent smile made her want to weep once more and bid for the comfort he so obstinately withheld.

"And if you were me, would you let your head rule your heart or the other way on?" she asked him.

He gave her a long, considering look before replying, and the lines of his face settled into the unrevealing mask he had worn in court. She was carried back to that day and the same sensation of impatience when he said with cool finality:

"That, in the circumstances, is a most improper question, Miss Hayes, and one I could not possibly answer with any certainty. You will have to make your own decisions, or, perhaps, Mr. Brown will make them for you."

"Perhaps he will!" she answered on a rising note of angry disappointment. "Perhaps he'll settle my doubts and everyone else's, too, once and for all . . . and — and whatever he proposes, I shall be only too happy to oblige him, so you needn't think a cold in the head will prevent me from keeping that appointment now."

"What appointment?" John Squires asked unexpectedly from the doorway. She had heard him arrive some time ago and make his way up to the nursery, and she turned to him now with relief at the interruption, but before she could reply Robert said with cool amusement:

"Haven't you heard the great news? Our little Victoria has been summoned at last to the Presence."

"Yes, Kate told me," the doctor answered rather curtly, turning a professional eye on the girl's flushed face and overbright eyes. "You look as if you're more in need of medical attention than that young man upstairs, Victoria. Are you running a temperature?"

"I don't know, but whether I am or not, nothing is going to stop me from going to London on Monday," she replied, and he gave Robert a shrewd, appraising glance, then said briskly:

"In that case, the sooner you're tucked up in bed the better, and I suggest that you stay there tomorrow if you want to be fit by Monday."

"Now that, Victoria," said Robert approvingly, "is an excellent notion. It will give you time to prepare for this momentous occasion and consider the various ways in which you might be expected to oblige Mr. Brown."

"Run along, now," John said, ignoring the interruption. "I'll be up in a little while to run the rule over you and prescribe something to tide you over the worst. Ah, here's Elspeth come to take charge with hot water bottles and a very determined expression, so away you go."

Victoria took herself off, and Robert got up and poured a couple of drinks, saying the doctor might as well refresh himself while he waited and John accepted the offer absently, then asked:

"Do you do it on purpose or don't you care?"

"Do what, for heaven's sake?"

"You know very well. Making fun of the poor child's obsession with her illusionary benefactor."

"But the gentleman's far from being illusionary, as the latest development should convince you."

"But Victoria's conception of him may well be. It would be a pity if your vagaries drive her to extremes."

"My vagaries?"

"For want of a better definition. It's none of my business, I suppose, but it isn't very kind to let an inexperienced girl take your attention seriously if you mean nothing more than a mild flirtation."

For a moment the icy anger which leapt into Robert's eyes and the hint of pain in the tightening of the muscles round his mouth took the doctor by surprise, but when he spoke his voice was quite controlled.

"As you say, it's none of your business," he anwered coldly, "and since we're being personal, I would suggest you take a hand in working out Kate's problems rather than mine."

"Since Kate is involved with your problems, and incidentally, with mine, you can hardly expect me to be indifferent," John retorted, and Robert's taut expression relaxed in surprise.

"But, my good chap! Surely you aren't labouring under the impression that Kate cherishes anything more than a cousinly fondness for me?" he exclaimed.

"I've never been sure, but Victoria certainly does," John replied a little stiffly, "and since she's a nice child with a strong sense of obligation it hasn't helped her to sort out her own emotions."

"Oh, dear, oh, lord! What very unnecesary complications!" Robert observed, sounding at once both rueful and relieved.

"If," John said, finishing his whisky and putting down the glass, "you had been a little more explicit instead of indulging in provocation there need have been no complications. I think perhaps I may have misjudged you, Farmer, in the matter of your intentions, but don't carry this little game too far. Young girls have curious ways of saving their pride and I fancy you might have a serious rival in Mr. Brown."

"Are you suggesting I should come clean, as the saying is, before allowing this eventful meeting to take its course?" asked Robert with a return to his rather sardonic manner, and the doctor shrugged and got to his feet.

"I would have thought it wise unless you have come to the conclusion that Mr. Brown would provide a convenient let-out," he said, but did not have the satisfaction of stirring up that flash of anger again.

"That, of course, is a point of view," Robert observed amicably. "Still, one must take chances in this life, mustn't one? It would hardly be fair to my possible rival to use persuasion before he's had a chance to reveal himself."

For a moment John did not speak but stood regarding the other man with hostile but puzzled eyes.

"You're a curious fellow," he said then. "I believe you're in love with that little girl after all. Why the hell don't you put your cards on the table and end all this Mr. Brown nonsense?"

"Because, nonsense or not, Mr. Brown has made his mark. Until she meets him Victoria will never be free of this image she has created for herself, and I prefer to compete with flesh and blood rather than an imagined father-figure."

"And if those proposed suggestions don't turn out to be strictly paternal?"

"My dear chap, your guess is as good as mine. Suppose we leave such contingencies until they materialise — and don't, I beg you, offer well-meaning as well as professional advice when you go upstairs."

"And what of the possibilities of coercion from another quarter? I doubt if your elderly rival will be quite so particular in view of past benefits," John retorted with some impatience. Robert merely shrugged and smiled a little enigmatically and the doctor turned on his heel.

"Well, I'll go up now and take a look at her," he said a shade gruffly, "after which I would like a word with Kate in private."

"Yes, you do that. I will diplomatically take myself off to the nursery and amuse my godson, so don't hurry away unless you have to," Robert said, observing with wry amusement the dull flush creeping up the back of the doctor's neck as he left the room.

After John had visited her, Victoria lay in her bed listening to the comings and goings in the house and trying to guess what they portended. She heard Robert come up to the nursery where he seemed to remain for some time and, later, Kate's voice on the stairs followed by the sharp little click the parlour door made when it was shut because the latch was faulty.

She must have dozed off, for the daylight was nearly gone when she heard John drive off. She hoped Kate would come up and tell her how he had taken the news, forgetting that there had been no chance as yet to have her own surmises confirmed, but Kate did not come.

She turned her face to the wall, feeling as she had at school when parents came down for special occasions and everybody seemed to have someone belonging except her. She remembered how Mr. Brown had gradually become a myth in whom no one believed very seriously, and her own hurt feelings at his continued disinterest. Well, she thought with renewed confidence, that was all changed now. Mr. Brown was not only about to declare himself, but clearly had definite plans for her future. It was distinctly comforting to know that although the Trust was coming to an end, it was possibly the beginning of a new relationship . . .

It was dark before anyone visited her. Elspeth had

brought up a light supper and remained for a while to chat, but her thoughts must have been elsewhere, for she answered at random and did not even notice that Victoria's wet clothes still lay in a sodden heap on the floor. When Kate finally came it was only to say good-night and enquire a little apologetically if there was anything she needed.

"How's Timmy?" Victoria asked, remembering that Kate must still hold her responsible for any harm that might have come to the boy, but Kate only laughed and replied rather absently that Timmy was making the most of his situation and she was afraid she had created rather a fuss about nothing.

"In fact, my cunning son seems to think he was rather clever to hide and give you a fright, because it would make you change your mind," she added, sounding suddenly mischievous, and Victoria sent her a puzzled glance. There was something different about Kate tonight; it was almost as if she was a schoolgirl again, nursing a secret which she had been forbidden to tell.

"Change my mind?" she said guardedly.

"About leaving us. I tried to explain about Mr. Brown, but he seems to think he's a kind of wizard who's put a spell on you, and in a sense, I suppose, he has. Poor Timmy! This will be his first lesson in playing second fiddle, but we all have to learn, don't we?"

Victoria eyed her uneasily. "Kate, you're being very unlike yourself. Have you something you want to tell me?"

"Nothing more momentous than a decision to adopt John's advice and keep you in bed tomorrow. Whatever happens you must keep that appointment on Monday."

Victoria blinked. It was Kate who had been suspicious, counselling postponement—and now here she was speeding on an eventual parting with uncomplimentary haste.

"You and Robert have come to an understanding, I imagine," she said tentatively, and Kate smiled.

"Oh yes. He's quite convinced me that the sooner you meet your peculiar patron, the better, and since he's going with you, I'm quite satisfied that you won't be persuaded into anything foolish."

It was not the answer Victoria wanted, but short of putting her question more bluntly she would have to be content to wait until Kate was ready to confide; but as if she had guessed her thoughts Kate sat down on the side of the bed and said suddenly:

"Victoria, you remember I told you I had been in love with another man before I married Jim?"

"Yes. He was engaged to someone else, so you did the noble thing and cut your losses, and when you both were free you met again. Well, I know all that, so what?" Victoria replied, trying to sound casual and adult and Kate smiled.

"But you don't, my dear. I only met him again quite by chance that week-end I was in London. He hadn't changed a bit, but thank goodness, I had. I thought you might like to know."

Victoria was silent from sheer surprise, then she remembered Elspeth's acid remark about bad pennies turning up again and her relief was mixed with pain.

"You thought it was Robert, didn't you?" said Kate softly.

"Did he tell you that?"

"I don't think he even suspected. No, John told me."

"Oh! Well, it's of no consequence now. I'm glad all the same, Kate, that I wasn't poaching. It worried me dreadfully."

"Silly child! Don't you think in the circumstances that you should reconsider before casting in your lot with Mr. Brown?"

Kate made the question sound like a casual afterthought, but her eyes were warm and a little anxious and Victoria had to fight an impulse to succumb to the luxury of confessing to the sorry state of her own heart, but it was too late now for reassurance, neither did she fancy the possibility that Robert might still be offering to make insulting amends.

"There's nothing to consider. I took too much for granted, that's all. It was really very fortunate that Robert's silly trick misfired," she said, and began to sneeze.

"Those blasted roses!" Kate exclaimed, getting up and smoothing down the bedcover. "Oh, well, perhaps the real

173

Mr. Brown will remedy that, once he's made his intentions plain. Would you like Robert to come up and say goodnight?"

"No!" Victoria answered so vehemently that she started coughing. Kate stood looking down at her with rather an odd expression, then she firmly tucked in the bedclothes and went away.

Victoria spent Sunday in feverish anticipation of the morrow. Fears that she might not be fit enough to travel were mixed with a sneaking desire for the opposite, for although her temperature was normal, there was no denying that her cold was in its most unbecoming stage. Robert had thoughtfully sent up a supply of masculine handkerchiefs and by the time he put in an appearance himself to enquire, her nose was pink from repeated blowing and she was inclined to be tearful.

"Isn't it too humiliating?" she said when he commiserated tactfully with her situation. "The only one time in my whole life that I want to make an impression and I have to look like a half-boiled rabbit!"

"Oh, hardly that . . . just a frail young thing with a regrettable addiction to the bottle," he replied gravely, making her giggle. "Your ears are pink too, which on second thoughts does suggest a rabbit on account of their size."

"You," she said, "are very rude, and it will serve you right if you catch my cold." She added rather casually: "I think after all, it might be better if I postponed that meeting tomorrow. It wouldn't be very tactful to pass on a cold to Mr. Brown as a token of esteem."

"Nonsense!" he retorted cheerfully. "Weren't you taught that procrastination is the thief of time? For all you know the poor old gentleman may be on his last legs and thinking of making his will. You surely wouldn't want to disappoint him after all this time?"

"There you go again—mocking at poor Mr. Brown!" she exclaimed, welcoming a bracing return of hostility. "Why do you always have to provoke me just when I'm trying to be friendly?"

"Possibly because I'm heartily sick and tired of Mr. Brown and all his works!" he replied. "You, I might add,

are surprisingly touchy on the subject, considering the gentleman in question is a stranger."

"Well, after tomorrow he won't be a stranger any more, so you can stop amusing yourself at my expense," she snapped, and his eyebrows rose with a quizzical air of indulgence.

"At Mr. Brown's expense, not yours, my purblind child," he said.

"Purblind?" she echoed between sneezes, and he took a clean handkerchief from the pile on the table beside her and tossed it into her lap.

"Yes, purblind," he said gently, "but there's some excuse for you, I'll admit. I tend to forget your youth and inexperience when we wrangle so merrily."

"Merrily?"

"Yes, merrily, and a good thing too. Relations would have become insupportable if there hadn't been a lighter side to our disputes. Now take your medicine and keep warm, and by tomorrow you'll feel more like putting on your best bib and tucker to dazzle Mr. Brown. When the interview is over I'll take you out to lunch to celebrate."

She saw no more of him until the evening when Kate thought it wise, in view of tomorrow's trip, to get dressed and join them for Sunday supper. Perhaps because John Squires had joined the party, Robert seemed to be in a mood to tease. Since he appeared to be accepting the doctor's presence with unusual equanimity, Victoria bore with his mischievous attentions for Kate's sake, but even Kate, who every so often exchanged knowing smiles with John, finally rounded on him and told him to behave.

"You can hardly accuse me of improper conduct while you and Squires provide such admirable chaperonage," he protested innocently, and she gave him a look that was strongly reminiscent of Elspeth.

"You know very well what I mean," she retorted briskly. "You're an expert at tripping up witnesses and getting them confused, but you're not in court now."

"Are you confused, Victoria Mary?" he enquired with mock anxiety, and Victoria who was beginning to long for the privacy and solace of her bed gave him a withering look.

"Not in the least," she replied, somewhat tartly. "Such confusion as I may once have felt was only to be expected since I was very green, and unaccustomed to charming insincerities, but things are crystal clear now, so you don't need to keep on pressing your point in this tedious fashion."

"Well said," the doctor murmured with an appreciative grin. "I think you asked for that, Farmer."

"Yes, perhaps I did," Robert answered, and his eyes were suddenly grave. Kate, looking surprised and a little unhappy, said rather quickly:

"Why don't we all play Consequences or something instead of talking a lot of nonsense?" Both John and Victoria smiled sympathetically though they did not second the suggestion, but Robert exclaimed irrepressibly:

"Now *that's* an idea! I haven't played Consequences since I was a boy. Think what fun we could have with sinister Mr. Brown meeting gullible Miss Hayes in a lonely wood. He said to her: 'How will you repay me for past favours'? She said to him—"

"That's enough!" Kate broke in quite sharply, but Victoria got to her feet and, looking Robert straight in the eye, finished for him:

"She said to him: 'In any way you choose that will settle affairs once and for all'. Now, if you don't mind, Kate, I'll say good-night and go to bed. I wouldn't want to keep Robert waiting in the morning."

She crossed the room and unhurriedly mounted the corner staircase which had played such an unhappy part in her affairs, and John remarked gravely: "I think she meant that. Are you trying to drive the child into the arms of a total stranger who may or may not be on the level, Farmer?"

"Perhaps," Robert answered with tantalising prevarication, and the doctor frowned impatiently. Kate touched his hand sympathetically, but she, too, seemed surprisingly unperturbed.

"Dear John," she murmured softly, "Robert isn't as hard-boiled as he sounds. Even if he goes about things in a peculiar fashion, he knows his own business best."

"Thanks, my comely cousin. I suggest we all have a

nightcap to restore relationships and talk of cabbages and kings," Robert said, and got up to dispense the drinks.

Victoria slept heavily as a result of her cold and the strain of standing up to Robert's provocations, and although Kate called her with a breakfast tray in plenty of time, she fell asleep again and was obliged to dress with more haste than she had planned for such a momentous occasion. Kate came back as she was trying to decide which dress to wear, thankful that the weather at least was being kind and she could dispense with the summer coat which had been chosen for utility rather than smartness.

"Would you think the candy-stripe pink or the black sheath? The print is gay and was quite expensive but the black is towny and more sophisticated," she said, her head on one side, but Kate took a navy-blue linen with crisp white collar and cuffs off its hanger and replied without thinking:

"No, wear this, it's Robert's favourite. He says it gives you the air of a demure schoolgirl which is most intriguing and reminds him of the day he first saw you in court."

"Well, that's a day *I* have no wish to remember, and since it's Mr. Brown I want to impress and not Robert, I'll wear the black," Victoria retorted, snatching back the dress and throwing it on the bed, but when later, she came downstairs, ready to go, Kate observed with amusement that she had evidently changed her mind. She thought the girl looked delightful in the plain navy dress which made her appear so incredibly slender, but she was too tactful to comment and merely observed that she approved of the broad headband which did duty for a hat and was distinctly becoming.

For a moment as they left, Victoria had a cold feeling of finality, the sensation of boats too hastily burnt, the point of no return too suddenly reached.

"It isn't really good-bye, is it, Kate?" she said as the older woman kissed her.

"Of course not, you goose! Robert will see you safely on to the train after lunch and Elspeth's preparing your favourite dinner."

"If, that is, Mr. Brown doesn't spirit her away to his hidden lair before she can change her mind," observed Robert from the open front door.

"Now, Rob, don't tease," Kate admonished him. "Pay no attention to him, Victoria, if he tries to provoke you all the way to London. He's probably only jealous of his unknown rival."

It was not very kind of Kate to make fun of her, too, Victoria thought as she followed Robert out to the waiting Bentley, but whatever his intentions may have been, he seemed undisposed for chatter. He drove with his usual speed and she sat beside him, every so often glancing at the hard, unrevealing lines of his profile and wondered what he was thinking about. Her own efforts at small talk having met with little response, she relapsed into an uneasy silence and wished she were not filled with so many last-minute doubts. Now that she was actually to come face to face with her benefactor she was aware of a strange reluctance. The mysterious Mr. Brown had been an accepted part of her background for so long that she had not paused to consider that one day there might be a reckoning. She remembered those other summonses to the office of Messrs. Chapple, Chapple & Ponsonby and her sharp disappointment at Mr. Brown's failure to appear. She would, she reflected unhappily, have been journeying to London today in a state of excited anticipation had it not been for the regrettable change in her situation. She wished Robert would make a last-minute appeal for further reflection before committing herself to the dictates of a stranger, but his disinclination to treat the subject seriously was even worse than his teasing and he seemed all at once like a stranger.

He braked violently to avoid a car which turned off without giving signals, swore under his breath, then gathered speed with fresh vigour, at the same time placing a hand on her knee.

"Nervous?" he asked.

"Not of your driving," she answered, edging away, and saw him smile with amused comprehension.

"Having cold feet for other reasons," he said, but his

178

tone was not conducive to a sympathetic hearing and she made no answer.

All too soon the country was left behind them and the Bentley was forced to a crawl as it joined the incoming stream of traffic. The rows of ugly little houses with their sooty gardens depressed Victoria unutterably and she thought with longing of the Sussex lanes and woods and the familiar grace of Farthings. How much longer would she have to think of the place as home after today's interview? she wondered disconsolately; what would be decided, had perhaps already been decided for her immediate future?

"I'm not, of course, obliged to agree to anything," she told herself reassuringly, aware too late that she had spoken aloud. She glanced a little nervously at Robert, hoping he had not heard, but he, with his usual promptness to pounce on an ill-considered remark, said a little mockingly:

"And what of those brave resolves of Saturday? Whatever your benefactor had in mind you would do your best to oblige him, you said. It's hardly becoming in a beneficiary to have second thoughts after accepting so much."

"You," she exclaimed, rejoicing in a temporary return to normal, "are the last person to preach gratitude and duty. If it hadn't been for you I wouldn't have been summoned to the Presence now."

"But that, surely was what you wanted," he pointed out with infuriating logic, and she gave an angry little bounce which shot her handbag on to the floor, spilling out its contents.

"Will you please shut up, Robert Farmer, or better still, let me out here and I'll take a bus," she said, diving under his legs for an escaping lipstick.

"That would make you late for your appointment, which wouldn't make a good impression — do stop fiddling about with my ankles, my dear child, you might cause an accident," he said, sounding inappropriately restored to good humour, and she surfaced once more, rather pink in the face.

"I was *not* fiddling about with your ankles — I was retrieving my lipstick, and if you had an ounce of decent feeling you'd be giving me a little c-confidence instead of s-slapping me down!" she retorted, and he glanced down at her with a quizzical little lift of one eyebrow.

"Are you in need of confidence, then, Victoria Mary?" he enquired quite gently, and she blinked rather rapidly and looked hastily out of the window.

"Naturally," she replied in slightly muffled tones. "It's most important that Mr. Brown should like me and — and I'm already handicapped by having a c-cold in the head."

"Poor Victoria! Never mind, you can have a good blow before we get there and powder your nose and I don't suppose anyone will notice a slight pinkness round the edges," he said.

After that they drove on in silence, but soon Victoria managed to ignore the slight sinking feeling in the pit of her stomach in renewing acquaintanceship with the exhilarating bustle of the London streets.

They were passing the Law Courts and she gazed upon them, remembering that last occasion when she had journeyed so expectantly on top of a bus to a meeting which had never taken place and had, instead, been packed off abroad to finish her education.

"Unpleasant memories?" asked Robert suddenly, as they waited in a traffic block, and because for the moment her thoughts were divorced from the immediate present she gave him that slow, lifting smile.

"Not all unpleasant," she answered. "I was thinking of the times I came this way expecing to meet Mr. Brown only to be fobbed off with a stuffy lawyer. Twice they sent for me and twice I was disappointed, but third time lucky, they say, so this must be it." She sneezed twice and suddenly looked anxious. "You don't think this is another let-down, do you, Robert? They wouldn't have come out with all those queer hints and suggestions if Mr. Brown wasn't going to turn up, would they?"

"Who knows what eccentric clients may think fit to do at the last minute?" he replied as the traffic moved on. "Anyway, we'll soon be there, so have a good blow and powder your nose and prepare yourself for the worst."

Robert parked the Bentley in an adjacent cul-de-sac behind the office premises and told Victoria to go on up while he locked the car. She hurried up the dark stair-case with its familiar musty smell, hoping that he was tactfully giving her time to make herself known without his supervision. She could hear his leisurely steps on the bottom stair just as she reached the top and quickly slipped into the outer office, letting the door swing shut behind her.

Like the recurrence of a dream the same old clerk came forward to meet her, a little greyer, a little more bent, but as primly incurious as he had appeared three years ago.

"Please take a seat, Miss Hayes, Mr. Brown has not yet arrived," he said, conveying a touch of reproof in that she herself was too early.

"Then he really *is* coming?" she said, aware that she had been half expecting excuses for unavoidable absence.

"Naturally," the old man replied with a slight air of disapproval, then allowed himself a fleeting expression of surprise as Robert opened the door and came in.

"Good morning, Mr. Farmer. Your appointment was for eleven-fifty-five, if I am not mistaken. Would you care to come back later?" he said.

"I know I'm early, but I don't mind waiting," Robert replied, sitting down on a hard, uncomfortable chair and stretching out his long legs before him.

"I will just ascertain whether Mr. Chapple is free," the clerk said, and Robert gave Victoria a most undignified wink as the old man knocked on the door of one of the private rooms and vanished inside.

"You needn't try to upset my dignity by making me giggle," Victoria said, sitting down on another hard chair. "Anyway, he hasn't arrived yet, so it looks as if you'll have a long wait for your own appointment. Wouldn't you like to take a walk and come back?"

"Not at all. I promised Kate to see you safely bestowed before attending to my own business. Besides, I'm not en-tirely devoid of curiosity concerning your Invisible Man," Robert replied, and gave her another rather disconcerting wink.

Before she had time to retort, the door opened and Mr.

Chapple came bustling out, rubbing his hands together and exuding an air of roguish bonhomie which forcibly reminded Victoria of their first meeting.

"Well, well, well! So you have already introduced yourselves," he said. "But of course I'm forgetting, Mr. Farmer, that you're a cousin of Mrs. Allen's, so you are hardly strangers to one another."

"Mr. Farmer drove me up from Sussex as he already had an appointment with you, but I don't mind waiting if you would care to see him first, as Mr. Brown hasn't yet arrived," Victoria said politely as she shook hands, hoping that Robert would take the hint and leave her to get over the first introductions alone.

For a moment Mr. Chapple looked surprised and a little put out as if he suspected an impertinence, then he caught Robert's eye, went a little red in the face and cleared his throat with a series of explosive little pops.

"Well, well, well . . ." he said again, ushering them towards his private room. "No need for hurry . . . no need at all . . . you must both of you wait in the greater comfort of my own office, so come along in. I have a very tolerable sherry decanted in honour of this occasion, so I trust you'll join me in a little celebration."

Victoria hung back, feeling slightly bewildered, but the two men were waiting for her to precede them and she could do no less than make the best of the situation. It seemed to her a little premature to start drinking before the principal participant had joined them, but Mr. Chapple was already handing round glasses and making coy little jokes which she thought ill became him, and Robert seemed to find nothing odd in the procedure.

"Well now, before we get to business, may I propose a toast to the—er—winding up of a project which I will confess caused me grave misgivings at the time. Mr. Farmer—Miss Hayes—I drink to the happy conclusion of this affair."

He raised his glass on the last words, took a slow, appreciative swallow and nearly choked when Victoria suddenly stamped her foot at him and burst out:

"It's all another hoax, after all! I don't know why you've staged this ridiculous scene, Mr. Chapple, unless you've

182

been put up to it by your learned friend who has, I've cause to know, a very odd sense of humour, but it wasn't very kind, was it, to pretend when you knew all the time Mr. Brown wouldn't be c-coming?"

Mr. Chapple's jaw dropped visibly and he favoured Robert with an outraged glance before turning an offended eye on Victoria, remembering his impressions at that first meeting. He had been prepared to admit on this occasion that judging by appearance, the experiment had paid off, but it seemed that Graham Hayes' daughter was no less likeable at twenty than she had been at fourteen.

"Well, upon my soul, young lady! A respectable firm of solicitors hardly lend themselves to the perpetrating of hoaxes!" he snapped. "It would seem that it is I who should demand explanations, not you."

Victoria had taken refuge in blowing her nose, thankful that her cold gave her an excuse for concealing a humiliating threat of tears. She heard Robert murmuring something she could not catch, followed by a dignified snort from Mr. Chapple, then the sound of a door opening and shutting. She turned slowly, thinking that Robert had gone, but he was still there, propped against Mr. Chapple's imposing desk and regarding her with a cool and unconcerned eye.

"Would you care for the loan of my handkerchief?" he asked conversationally. "Your own doesn't appear to be very adequate."

"No, I wouldn't," she replied ungraciously. "Why are you still here?"

"To keep an appointment," he replied with the indulgent air of an adult humouring a child.

"Your appointment was for a quarter to twelve and has nothing to do with mine, anyway," she pointed out, wondering at the same time, what could be occupying Mr. Chapple's attention.

"Hasn't it?"

"Well, only in a nosey kind of way, but as Mr. Brown isn't here, your curiosity will have to go unsatisfied, won't it?"

"Who says he isn't here? Not poor old Chapple dispensing bonhomie and his best sherry. You really did cut him to the quick with those most improper suggestions."

She stared at him dumbly for a moment, only conscious that she might have jumped too hastily to conclusions and it would be just like Mr. Robert Farmer to have the last laugh.

"You mean he's gone to fetch him?" she said, then. "He was here all the time, waiting in another room?"

"Here all the time, certainly, but not waiting in another room. Can't you guess, Victoria Mary?" he replied, and, had she not known him so well, Victoria could have sworn he seemed suddenly anxious.

"What are you trying to tell me? That you've thought up another good practical joke for your entertainment?" she said, clinging to proved facts, but her voice was not as steady as she would have wished and her legs felt suddenly as if they were made of cotton-wool.

"No joke, I assure you," he replied rather wryly. "Neither were those perishing roses a joke, since they really did come from Mr. Brown. Aren't you ever going to forgive me for that?" he said, and for a moment the room seemed to spin round her and the rows of deed-boxes looked in imminent danger of falling on her head.

"I think I'd better sit down," she said, groping wildly for the nearest chair. Robert said nothing but poured out some more sherry and placed her fingers firmly round the glass. She took a long swallow while the room slowly righted itself, then blinked up at him propped once more against the desk and regarding her with tender amusement.

"Are you disappointed?" he asked, and she took a deep breath.

"That Mr. Brown turns out to be only you? I suppose, knowing the peculiar way your mind works, I should have guessed there was something fishy going on," she retorted, recapturing her self-possession with an aplomb that made him smile.

"Something fishy? Oh, surely not."

"Yes—decidedly fishy if I'd stopped to think. Mr. Brown, always so adamant on the subject of jobs and possible admirers, showed a remarkable tolerance where you were concerned. In fact, though he set his face firmly against followers, he never took exception to you."

"Well, naturally one tends to be broadminded where one's own interests are concerned," he replied, quite unabashed, and she looked at him wrathfully.

"Then the whole thing was engineered from the start —Kate offering me the only job I was allowed to accept, you coming down to find out how your experiment was working—no wonder I never had a chance to make a life of my own! I suppose Kate was in on the joke, even if she did play up to the extent of sacking me."

"Kate knew nothing until yesterday when, in view of pending change, it seemed only right to put her in the picture. She was aware that I had retained an interest in Graham Hayes' daughter and was glad to offer you a job on my recommendation, but it never crossed her mind that the invisible Mr. Brown and her by no means invisible cousin could be one and the same person."

"Why did you do it? Make yourself responsible for a stranger you had only seen in the witness-box, I mean?" she asked curiously, and he ran a hand absently over his lean jaw as if unsure of the answer.

"I don't really know," he said then. "There was something about you that stuck in my mind and produced quite irrational feelings of remorse since my cross-examination was wholly justified . . . there was no one to pick up the pieces and I had an impulse to play providence . . . perhaps because I'd been let down myself and was in the mood for a little gratitude . . . who knows on looking back what prompts one to certain actions? It may be that I was no less eccentric and careless of my money than Mr. Brown appeared to be . . . it could, I suppose be judged the height of eccentricity to go to such lengths to provide oneself with a suitable marriage partner."

She stared at him disbelievingly, not very sure if he wasn't still enjoying a private joke at her expense, and he added with sudden gentleness: "Don't look so incredulous . . . that, to you, must seem an unromantic way of going about things, but as I'd fallen out of love with a rather resounding crash, it seemed quite sensible then to insure against the future."

"I see. Wrapping the next possible contender in cotton wool until you were ready."

His smile was a little wry and he momentarily hunched his shoulders as though he felt a draught from the open window.

"Well, not quite so cold-blooded as that, and I was always prepared for my plans miscarrying, hence the cotton wool. You see, my child, as I once told you, even browbeating barristers have their pipe-dreams, and there was no more harm in my fantasies than in yours relating to Mr. Brown."

She considered this gravely, then said with that sudden capitulation to reason which always surprised him:

"No, there wasn't, was there? I don't in any case, see anything odd in wanting to fashion someone to your specification should the opportunity arise. The only thing is one's dreams don't always work out as one expects. Look how I've been let down by Mr. Brown."

"Very true, if all you expected was a substitute papa who would make no embarrassing demands, which brings us back to the point of this long-delayed meeting," Robert said with a sudden alarming change of manner and, sitting down in the chair Mr. Chapple reserved for interviewing clients fixed her with a cool, forensic eye. "However mistaken you were in your private fantasies, the fact remains, Miss Hayes, that you made certain statements before witnesses which I now propose to hold you to."

"What statements?"

"You know very well. In return for past considerations, you were willing to oblige Mr. Brown to the best of your ability."

"Well, I didn't know he was you, then," Victoria protested indignantly, but she felt herself colouring as she remembered Robert's outrageous suggestions and her own rash commitments.

"The fact of his identity makes no difference," he replied with something of his courtroom manner, and she blinked but was not silenced.

"Yes, it does. You obtained that assurance under false pretences, so it cancels out!" she said with renewed confidence, and he grinned, suddenly shedding his legal mask.

"A good try, but it won't hold water. The fact that your unknown patron happens to be me and not a gouty

186

old gentleman with slightly improper intentions in no way alters the case. That you were prepared to meet the demands of a total stranger as a means of escape from me in no way releases you from obligation, so hadn't we better end this farce once and for all? Old man Chapple will be back any minute to offer congratulations and draw up contracts."

"Draw up c-contracts?"

"Figuratively speaking, of course, since I trust that will be the vicar's privilege. Still and all, it might be as well to have everything down in writing in case you're thinking of ratting on the agreement."

"There hasn't *been* an agreement!" she shouted at him, nearly in tears. "What are you trying to do to me, Robert? Get your own back because I turned you down? You know very well you have only yourself to thank for that. I could hardly be expected to take you seriously after your silly prank with the roses."

His eyebrows went up in that familiar expression of fastidious enquiry.

"I thought I'd explained away that bone of contention," he remarked. "Don't you understand that I wasn't ready then to confess to a dual personality, neither were you in a mood to take kindly to relinquishing those father-figure fantasies. I'm prepared to fill that role upon occasions, but not to the exclusion of the normal demands of the flesh. Did you really think I asked you to marry me as a kind of consolation prize?"

"It wouldn't have been any c-consolation, so you needn't f-flatter yourself," she flung back at him, and quite suddenly found herself in tears.

He was round the desk and kneeling beside her chair before she even had time to turn away.

"There, my poor bedevilled sweetheart . . . stop fighting me . . . it's a losing battle, you know," he murmured as he gathered her into his arms. "You try so hard to convince me you couldn't care less, but you're forgetting those revealing letters to Mr. Brown."

"You did read my letters, then?"

"Every one. Such stiff, dutiful little effusions, Victoria

187

Mary Hayes — until that last *cri de coeur* which certainly gave me encouragement."

"Why did you never answer?"

"I don't really know—unless it was a reluctance to shatter the paternal image which you seemed to set such store by. Now, will you please dry your eyes and attend to me seriously? I can't offer better proof of sincerity than to propose once more on my bended knee, so please, dear, militant Victoria Mary, don't send me away again with a flea in my ear."

She began to smile at him, but tears and a cold in the head stifled responses and she snatched the handkerchief from his breast pocket and blew her nose with some violence.

"Do get up, Robert," she said then, clutching at the remnants of her composure. "It doesn't become you at all to kneel and be humble."

"No? But then you've still a great deal to learn about me, haven't you—between the traditional browbeatings, of course," he said, but he obediently got to his feet, pulling her up with him. "You haven't answered me, yet."

"If you're really sure—" she began a little shyly, and he gave her a shake.

"Of course I'm sure. I've been sure ever since that day in the orchard when you thought you'd fooled me and stood under an apple tree shaking down blossom and stealing my heart away."

"Did I? Did I really, Robert—as long ago as that?"

"Yes, you did, and merely disliked me intensely in return, which was ungenerous of you."

"You could hardly expect me to feel kindly towards you in the circumstances," she pointed out, and he grinned.

"Well, no—perhaps you have a point there. You still haven't answered me or, for the matter of that, given me any assurance of a return of affection."

"I don't need to—I told Mr. Brown," she answered demurely, and he grinned again.

"So you did. Well, I suppose I must be content with that for the time being. At least you no longer labour under delusions concerning Kate!"

"Kate?" For the moment she had forgotten Kate and her eyes grew troubled.

"No," she said. "She explained about that other man, only you couldn't very well turn her and Timmy out of Farthings, could you, Robert?"

"Oh, I see. Without the bribe of Farthings, you'd think twice before committing yourself," he countered so severely that she looked quite horrified, then he laughed and pinched her ear. "You don't need to worry about Kate's future, you prevaricating goose! I fancy it won't be very long before the worthy doctor succeeds in persuading her to move down to the village."

The last remaining scruple melted away and her face lit up.

"Oh, I'm so *glad!* John is so kind and dependable and he'll make a far better stepfather than you ever would!" she exclaimed, and he gave her another shake.

"Very possibly," he replied dryly. "For myself, I prefer to father and bring up my own brats than be a stand-in for someone else's."

"Yes," she agreed a little smugly, "it wouldn't suit you at all to play second fiddle."

"No, it wouldn't, so please remember that in the future, Miss Hayes. No followers, however respectable, or there'll be trouble."

"You see?" she said as he bent his head at last to kiss her. "I'll never quite get away from Mr. Brown. He had very old-fashioned views about followers."

"Oh, damn Mr. Brown and his old-fashioned views! I'll have enough to contend with without that gentleman being thrust down my throat when it suits!" Robert exclaimed, and tilted up her face to his with some impatience.

"You'll catch my cold," she murmured, and he administered one last shake before imprisoning her firmly between his hands.

"Don't change the subject," he said severely, and proceeded to ensure her silence for quite some time.

"Isn't it strange?" she said when finally she could speak, peering over his shoulder at the gloomy rows of deedboxes which probably held secrets and even scandals long since forgotten. "It all began in this ugly musty room and now it all ends here . . . do you suppose records of the Hayes Trust are buried in one of those boxes?"

"Most certainly, since this is a most reliable and trustworthy firm, but don't let skeletons in cupboards rattle their bones at you, sweetheart. Remember that sinister Mr. Brown has already been written off as only a bogle to frighten the bairns with," Robert said, ignoring a discreet tap on the door.

"He said to her: 'How will you repay me for past favours?' " Victoria murmured.

"And kindly remember the lady's reply," he promptly retorted. "What a pity we never got as far as the consequence."

"The immediate consequence will probably be an explosion from Mr. Chapple if you don't tell him to come in," Victoria retorted as a more peremptory knock sounded on the door and she straightened his tie with a proprietorial air before putting a decorous distance between them.

THE END